ILLUMINATION PRESENTS

Dr. Seuss'

The GRINCH

THE STORY OF THE MOVIE

ILLUMINATION PRESENTS
Dr. Seuss'
The
GRINCH
THE STORY OF THE MOVIE

Adapted by David Lewman
Based on the screenplay written by
Tommy Swerdlow and Michael LeSieur
and based on Dr. Seuss characters
owned and licensed by
Dr. Seuss Enterprises, L.P.

HarperCollins *Children's Books*

First published in the USA by Random House Children's Books in 2018
Simultaneously published in Great Britain by HarperCollins *Children's Books* in 2018
HarperCollins *Children's Books* is a division of HarperCollins*Publishers* Ltd,
HarperCollins Publishers
1 London Bridge Street
London SE1 9GF

The HarperCollins website address is
www.harpercollins.co.uk
1

ISBN 978-0-00-828830-3

Printed and bound in England by CPI Group (UK) Ltd, Croydon, CR0 4YY

MIX
Paper from
responsible sources
FSC™ C007454

This book is produced from independently certified FSC™ paper
to ensure responsible forest management.

For more information visit: www.harpercollins.co.uk/green

1

Far past any place you've ever been, surrounded by snowy mountains and deep forests, was a beautiful, wonderful town – a town like no other.

Who-ville.

Who-ville was a happy, friendly place full of happy, friendly *Whos*. But there was one time of year when *Who*-ville became even *happier*, with festive decorations and music everywhere. In the weeks before Christmas, the *Whos* rushed around *Who*-ville buying presents, bows, glitter, wrapping paper and delicious food for their family feasts. On street corners,

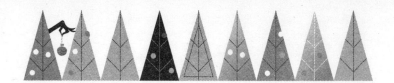

Whos handed out green wreaths and striped candy canes, made fresh right on the spot.

Lots of fresh, sparkling white snow fell on *Who*-ville all through the wintertime, and the *Whos* loved it! They rode snow-bikes to work. They skied. They sledged. They skated. They made snowmen. A special machine even cranked out snowballs by the dozens for snowball fights.

Yes, the *Whos* down in *Who*-ville liked Christmas a lot.

But the Grinch, in his cave north of *Who*-ville, did NOT!

The Grinch's cave towered high above *Who*-ville, up on Mt. Crumpit. A winding trail towards it was crowded with signs that read:

The Grinch did NOT like visitors.

Through twisted iron gates stood a door carved into the side of the mountain. Through that door, in a well-furnished cave with a maze of rooms and chambers, lived the grumpy green Grinch and his faithful little dog, Max.

On the snowy winter morning of 20 December, the Grinch lay in bed under a pile of thick blankets, snoring. It was five days before Christmas – a fact that the Grinch had been doing his very best to ignore.

The clock radio on the Grinch's chest of drawers clicked from 6:59 to 7:00. The radio began to play a loud and jolly song.

The Grinch's eyes popped open. Groaning, he stretched his furry green hand out from underneath the blankets and found a stack of books on his bedside table. He picked one up and threw it across the room at the radio. *WHOMP!*

But the radio just kept playing. Now a different, even jollier, even LOUDER Christmas tune was playing.

The Grinch threw a tennis racquet at the radio. *WHACK!* The station changed to one playing yet another Christmas song.

Enraged, the Grinch finally threw a lamp at the clock radio, knocking it off the drawers and into a deep crevice in the rock. "Humph," said the Grinch. But just as he gave a satisfied little smile . . .

. . . the tinny notes of a festive tune drifted up from the rocky depths. It was still playing.

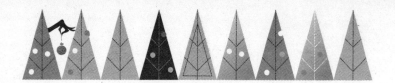

The Grinch sighed. "MAX!" he yelled. He yanked a rope next to his bed. Bells rang out through the cave. *DING-A-LING-A-LING!*

Max woke up right away. His master needed him! Tail wagging, he got to work making the Grinch's morning cup of coffee.

Max did ALL the household chores, and the cave was full of pulleys and levers to help him. He now ran up some steps to a small platform, pushing the plunger down into a coffee pot to fill a cup. With a measuring jug gripped tightly between his teeth, Max poured steamed milk to draw a frowny face on top of the Grinch's coffee. Just how the boss liked it!

With the coffee carefully balanced on a tray on top of his head Max backed into a mini-lift. He pulled down on a handle, and the creaky old lift slowly carried him up to the Grinch's bedroom.

DING! The lift door swung open and Max stepped out, careful not to spill a drop of the coffee.

Groaning and grunting, the Grinch took the hot drink, stood up and slid his feet into his slippers. He slowly walked to the bathroom, accompanied by the distant sound of Christmas songs playing from the bottom of the dark cavern. He grimaced.

"A shower's just the thing to drown out that racket," he growled.

The Grinch lingered a while in the shower, trying to forget about Christmas. When he stepped out, a blow-dryer turned on automatically, fluffing him up like a dandelion clock. He walked through a frame lined with bristles which brushed his fur and smoothed it down.

Meanwhile, Max scurried into the Grinch's wardrobe to fetch his master's outfit for the day. Using his mouth, he tugged the cord to turn on the wardrobe light. Then he flipped through all the pairs of green trousers on labelled hangers. The labels read:

BAD DAY

DISGRUNTLED

GRUMPY

MISERABLE

NASTY

VERY MISERABLE

WRETCHED

Max pondered the selection. With Christmas so near, the choice was obvious: VERY MISERABLE. Max pulled the trousers

off the hanger and handed them to the Grinch, who snapped them on. *SNAP!*

Looking in the mirror, the Grinch used a finger to swirl up the curly tuft of green fur on the top of his head, saying, "Boop!" He swirled Max's tuft up, too. "Boop!" Max wagged his tail.

Now he looked his very best (or indeed, worst), the Grinch was ready for the day ahead. But first, breakfast!

The Grinch crossed his bedroom and plopped down into a big red chair under an opening in the ceiling. His weight triggered a spring that lifted the chair up through the hole and into the dining room. He arrived right at his place at the table.

Max, who had already hurried up to the dining room, yanked another rope. This rope snaked through a system of pulleys that lifted the cover off the Grinch's plate.

"Ooh, I am starving!" the Grinch said, leaning forward to see what delicious dish Max had prepared for his breakfast. He blinked.

Sitting on the plate was a single bean.

2

The Grinch turned to Max for an explanation. "What is this?" he demanded.

"Arf! Arf! Arf!" Max barked.

"No, no, no, no," the Grinch said, shaking his head. "That's impossible! We can't be out of food!"

He ran to the kitchen. Every cupboard he flung open was empty. "Where's my personal reserve of Moose Juice and Goose Juice?" he cried. "My emergency stash of *Who* Hash? And my secret slew of frozen Beezle-Nut Stew?"

The Grinch stared at the empty shelves. "I specifically bought

enough food to last until January!" He patted his stomach guiltily. "How much comfort eating have I been doing?"

The cupboard containing Max's dog food was also empty. Max's tummy rumbled loudly and he stared at the Grinch with his big eyes.

The Grinch held up his hands, protesting, "No, I won't. I will not." He folded his arms across his chest stubbornly. "I am not going to *Who*-ville during Chrrr . . ." He struggled to spit out the word he hated so much. "Chrisss . . . argh! Chrrriii . . . Christmas! Ugh!"

Max nudged his empty food bowl towards the Grinch.

"Fine," he said at last. "But I'm going to despise every second of it."

Oh, the Grinch HATED Christmas! And he especially hated *Who*-ville at Christmas time. No one knew why, but the rumour was that his heart was two sizes too small.

As the wind howled and sleet blew, the Grinch and Max trudged through the twisted iron gates and headed down Mt.

Crumpit into *Who*-ville. The Grinch's long red-and-white-striped scarf flapped around his neck in the bracing breeze.

In *Who*-ville, it was a busy, bustling morning. The whole town was covered in Christmas decorations, making it look as though it had been built out of gingerbread. Every shop window, every street lamp and every bench was decked out with garlands and tinsel. The place positively glowed with good cheer and excitement.

A bus pulled up to a stop, and the driver leaned out to greet one of the waiting *Whos*. "Hey, Ted!" the driver called out in a friendly voice.

"Morning!" Ted said as he climbed aboard. Other passengers behind him said their cheerful good mornings as the doors closed and the bus pulled away from the snowy curb. *VROOM!*

Down the street, Donna *Who* saw the bus moving away. She was going to miss it! "Wait!" she shouted, beginning to run. "Wait, hold the bus!" She dodged other *Whos* on the pavement as she ran. "Excuse me. Sorry. Coming through!"

Sam, the driver, finally heard Donna yelling outside. "Oh!"

he said when he saw her. He stopped the bus straight away and opened the doors.

"Oof!" Donna grunted as she tripped and fell in the snow beside the bus. She picked herself up and climbed the steps, brushing snow off her coat and trousers.

"Sorry, Donna," the driver apologised.

"That's okay, Sam," she replied. "Thanks for stopping! Phew!"

Under her winter coat, Donna had on the medical scrubs she wore for her job as a nurse. She dug out coins and dropped them in the fare box. *DING! DING! DING!*

"They've still got you on night shifts, huh?" Sam asked.

"Sure do," Donna answered, nodding.

"Oh, by the way," Sam said, "Cindy-Lou forgot her hockey stick."

"Of course she did," Donna said, smiling. "That's my girl." Sometimes Donna thought her daughter would forget her own nose if it weren't attached to her face. Especially in the days just before Christmas when all the excitement seemed to push everything else out of her head.

As he and Max reached the edge of town, the Grinch sang to himself gloomily, "Jingle bells, Christmas smells, make it go away! Dee dee da, dee dee dee da . . ."

Trying to avoid all the holiday cheer, he hurried past the decorated shops and the *Whos* in their colourful jumpers with his head down. But four *Whos* singing Christmas carols spotted the elusive Grinch and followed him through the town, determined to serenade him.

The Grinch screamed and ran!

3

Breathing hard, the Grinch ducked into the town's general store. *DING!* A cheerful bell rang as he pushed the door open. A friendly *Who* shop assistant smiled and greeted the Grinch warmly. "Oh, hello! Happy Christm—"

The Grinch held up a finger to stop him. "Nuh-uh," he interrupted sharply, cutting off the assistant's Christmas wishes.

Moving down the aisles of the shop the Grinch quickly scooped can after can of *Who* Hash into a little wagon Max was pulling. He was in a foul mood, surrounded by cheerful *Whos* buying their Christmas nonsense. Perhaps he'd try a little sabotage . . .

He turned the corner into a new aisle and passed a shopper who was staring at the shelves of food. While the *Who* wasn't looking, the Grinch snatched a jar of spicy pickles out of her basket. He unscrewed the lid, pulled out a pickle and shoved the whole thing into his mouth. Then he made a disgusted face. "Blech!"

He spat the pickle back into the jar, screwed the lid back on, and dropped the jar into another *Who's* basket!

He passed another shopper who was trying to reach a jar on a high shelf. She stood on her tiptoes, stretching her arms. The taller Grinch reached round her and plucked the jar off the shelf. "Eh, what's this?" he sniffed, reading the label.

"Ooh!" the lady *Who* exclaimed. "Excuse me." She tapped the Grinch on the shoulder and he turned to look at her. The lady pointed at the jar. "Are you getting that? I need it for my Christmas stuffing."

"Hmm," mused the Grinch, looking at her. "No." Smiling, he put the jar back on the high shelf where she couldn't possibly reach it. Then he walked away.

How rude! "Well!" said the lady, shocked. "That's not very nice."

Then before he reached the end of the aisle, the Grinch gave the shelf a sharp bump with his elbow. The jar tottered, tipped, fell and shattered on the floor. *CRASH!*

"Oh, sugarplum!" the lady *Who* wailed.

The Grinch chuckled. This day was looking up.

In her kitchen, Donna *Who* stood by the sink, trying to unclog it with a toy arrow. She held a telephone between her ear and her shoulder as she struggled.

"I just got off the night shift," she told her friend on the other end of the line. "I have a list of errands a mile long, AND the babysitter left the kitchen sink clogged up."

Donna finished her phone call then called to her daughter, "Cindy-Lou, sweetheart, come and eat!"

"Coming!" Cindy-Lou answered.

The kettle started to whistle loudly from the stove. *TWWEEEEE!* "All right," Donna said, turning from the sink to move it off the stove. As she opened a bag of bread, she noticed her son Buster teething on his twin brother, Bean's, head. "Buster,

we've talked about this," she reminded him. "Your brother's head is not breakfast."

She tossed a couple of bread slices in the toaster, then set bowls of cereal in front of her twin boys. They turned up their noses at once. "Blech!" Buster said, sticking out his tongue.

Exhausted, Donna slumped over the sink for a moment. Just then, her daughter, Cindy-Lou popped through the door bundled up for the cold weather, her blonde hair braided into two long pigtails tied in bows. She had blue eyes, a big smile and almost everything she wore was pink. In her hand she clutched an envelope.

"Are you all right, Mum?" asked Cindy-Lou.

Donna forced a smile. "Yes! Never better!" She pointed to the sink. "What'd you put down here, anyway? A roller skate?"

"No," Cindy-Lou replied. "Just batter. Me and Mrs Wilbur made cookies."

"Oh, that explains it," Donna said. "Come and have some eggs."

"I can't," Cindy-Lou said, "I have to go and post something. But I made the beds and put away the twins' toys."

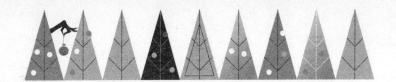

"Thanks, sweetheart," Donna said, smiling. "You didn't have to do that."

Cindy-Lou shrugged. She liked helping her mum. "I don't mind." She sniffed the air. "Something's burning."

"Just a second, sweetie," Donna said, turning her attention to the twins. "Bean, don't feed your brother with your feet!"

"Mum, the toast!" Cindy-Lou cried as black smoke rose from the toaster.

"I've got it!" Donna said. She popped the singed slices out, and set them in front of the twins. The boys grabbed the toast and happily chomped away.

"I'll be back soon, Mum!" Cindy-Lou said, turning to leave.

"Wait," Donna said. "Where are you going, again?"

"I told you," Cindy-Lou said, waving the envelope. "To post a letter."

"Okay, but just come here first," Donna said, stretching out her arms.

"Mum, I've got to go," Cindy-Lou insisted. Then she relented. "All right," she sighed. She went to her mum, who hugged her and kissed her forehead.

"Okay," Donna said. "Now you can go."

"Thanks, Mum!" said Cindy-Lou as she hurried out. "Bye, Buster! Bye, Bean!"

"Don't do anything I wouldn't do!" Donna called after her.

"Roger that, Mum!" Cindy-Lou said as she went out of the door.

4

Outside, Cindy-Lou jumped on her inflatable pink snow tube and zipped downhill. "Wooo!" she whooped as she picked up speed. "Here goes Cindy-Lou *Who*," she said, putting on her best sports commentator voice, "as she dashes through the snow with a very important letter!"

Down at the base of the hill Cindy-Lou spotted the postman driving his dogsled towards the postbox.

"Oh no!" Cindy-Lou cried. "I'm going to miss the post!"

"Shortcut!" she said, making a quick decision. She leaned forward on her snow tube and made a sharp turn. "Go, go, go, go!"

Cindy-Lou blasted through the blowing snow, leaning as far forward as she dared. *WHOOSH!* She hit a small hill that launched her into the air. "Whoooaaah!" she yelled.

WHUMP! Cindy-Lou landed on the roof of a house, slid across it and bounced on to the roof of the next house. Spinning and twirling, she was going faster and faster. "Whoa, whoa, whoa!" she shouted.

WHOMP! She hit the ground and slid right through the open front door of a house! "Uh oh," she muttered. She passed through the dining room, where a family of *Whos* were finishing up their breakfast.

"*Bon appétit!*" she said cheerfully to the surprised *Whos* as she slid out of the back door and into the garden. She hit another small slope, which sent her flying back up into the air. "Woo-hoo!" she whooped.

Just then, a gust of wind snatched the envelope out of her hand. "Oh no!" she cried, watching it blow away. There was no way for her to turn around. In fact, she couldn't even stop! Her snow tube didn't have any brakes. She just kept zooming through *Who*-ville, picking up even more speed. "Whoooaah!" Cindy-Lou screamed.

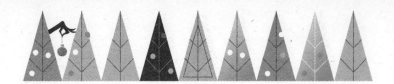

"Aaaaaaah!" She spotted the fluttering envelope as it was carried by the winter wind – it was heading in the same direction as she was. If only she could stop!

Near the postbox, the Grinch and Max crossed the street with the wagon full of shopping. Cindy-Lou's eyes widened, as she realised she was going to run right into them! "Watch out!" she cried.

"Ahhh!" yelled the Grinch.

WHAM! Cindy-Lou crashed into the Grinch, knocking him into a snowbank.

"Ooof!" the Grinch grunted. "Gaah. Uggh!"

He raised his head and spat snow out of his mouth. "PTOOO!"

Cindy-Lou crawled around on all fours, frantically searching the snow for her missing envelope. "No!" she cried. "My letter!"

"What is wrong with you?!" demanded the Grinch as he slowly got back to his feet. "Didn't you see me?" He pulled at the pink snow tube that had somehow become wrapped round him in the collision. "I mean, if this thing were a sledge, I'd . . . I'd . . . well, I'd be a goner!"

"I'm very sorry for bumping into you, truly I am, but this is

really important," said Cindy-Lou, looking at the Grinch as he freed himself from her snow tube. "Have you seen my letter? It's in an envelope. And it would have come falling down out of the sky. After I dropped it."

She resumed searching the snowy ground around them. Looking disgusted, the Grinch turned to Max and said, "And that right there is the true nature of the *Who* child. Always going straight back to 'me, me, me, my letter, me, me, me'."

Cindy-Lou shook her head. "No," she insisted, "you don't understand. This isn't just a letter. This is *the* letter!"

Her explanation failed to impress the Grinch.

"Oh, really," he said sarcastically. "Let me guess." He looked Cindy-Lou up and down, as if he were searching for clues. "Small child. On the twentieth December. Rabidly searching for a 'really important' lost letter." He stroked his chin and looked up to the sky, pretending to think. "Might this letter contain your list of greedy demands to Santa?"

Cindy-Lou stood up, offended. She pulled herself up to her full height and looked the Grinch in the eye. "First of all," she said, "I'm not that small. And second of all, they're not demands.

It's more like a wish, and what I'm wishing for is really, really important!"

The Grinch raised his eyebrows. "Well, then why send a letter?" he asked sarcastically. "I mean, if it's really that important you should just ask Santa face to face!" He pretended to remember something. "Oh, but that's right – no one's ever seen him. My bad." He turned to his dog. "Come on, Max. Let's get out of here."

As the Grinch and Max walked off, Cindy-Lou watched them go. "Bye, doggy," she said to Max, who wagged his tail.

The letter floated out of the sky and landed at Cindy-Lou's feet. She stared down at it, her thoughts full of what the Grinch had said.

5

As they headed back to Mt. Crumpit, the Grinch and Max passed the home of a bushy-bearded *Who* wearing a green hat and a red jumper with green Christmas trees on it. The *Who* was busy decorating his house, and, as he worked, he sang random words to different Christmas carols, "Hum-de-dum-dum Christmas . . . dah-de-dah-dah . . . mistletoe . . . It's de dum dum dum dum dum . . ."

"Whoa!" the Grinch said when he spotted the *Who*. "There he is, Max!" he said in a low voice. "The happiest *Who* alive, the

unbearable Bricklebaum!" Out of the side of his mouth, he told Max, "He thinks we're friends."

The Grinch ducked out of sight. He peered round a tree, watching Bricklebaum putting up what seemed to be miles of Christmas lights. The Grinch found the whole gaudy spectacle disgusting.

"Have a la-la-la-la Christmas," Bricklebaum kept singing loudly. "It's de dum dum dum dum dum . . ."

"He's not looking," the Grinch said to Max. "Quick, let's make a run for it!"

Looking for an opening, the Grinch watched as Bricklebaum climbed a ladder to the roof of his house. The roof was crammed full of lights, candy canes and a giant Santa's sleigh complete with eight plastic reindeer. There were even MORE lights along the gutters. All the electrical cords for these creations ran to a master switch. Cords also led to inflatable Christmas characters down in the garden: a penguin, a Santa Claus, giant presents and a teddy bear.

The Grinch pressed up against the tree that he and Max were hiding behind. "Go, go, go, go, go!" he hissed to Max.

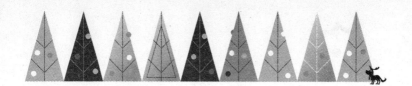

"What?" Bricklebaum said, looking around. "What was that?" But he didn't see anyone. He turned back to his work, resuming his singing, ". . . say hello and mistletoe and ho ho ho ho ho!"

The Grinch and Max made a mad dash for it . . . just as Bricklebaum hit the master switch to turn on the decorations. The huge Christmas characters began to inflate, and the Grinch wove between them with Max following with the wagon full of shopping. They were almost clear when—

WHAP! An inflatable snowman rose up as it filled with air. Its arm sprang out and smacked the Grinch in the face, knocking him right into the wagon. He ended up sprawled face-down in the snow. "Augh! Oof!"

"Oh, my goodness, Mr Grinch!" Bricklebaum cried. "I'm coming!" He scrambled down his ladder.

The Grinch lifted his head dizzily and shook snow off his face. He got up and started gathering the scattered shopping as fast as he could, hoping to escape before the friendly *Who* arrived to help.

"Leave Mr Grinch alone!" Bricklebaum told the inflatable

snowman as he rushed past. When he reached the Grinch, Bricklebaum said, "That's one tough balloon that you're fighting there. Here, come on. Let me help you."

"I do not want or need your help," the Grinch protested.

But Bricklebaum started picking up the shopping and putting it back on the overloaded little wagon. He paused, looking at one item. "Hair dye?" he said, laughing as he read the label. "'Gorgeous Green Goddess'!"

"Oh!" the Grinch exclaimed, snatching the hair dye out of Bricklebaum's hand.

"Hey, I'm sorry if I made you uncomfy," Bricklebaum said. "We all have to keep the grey away. I myself use 'Chocolate Explosion'. . ."

"You know what?" the Grinch interrupted as he buried the hair dye at the bottom of the wagon. "If you want to apologise, apologise for THAT!" He pointed an accusing green finger at Bricklebaum's overly decorated house. "You're a grown man with a life-size Santa's sleigh on your roof!"

"Don't blame me!" Bricklebaum said. "Haven't you heard? The mayor of *Who*-ville wants Christmas to be three times bigger this

year! That means three times the lights! Three times the eggnog! Three times the—"

"Information needed," the Grinch snapped.

Bricklebaum just laughed again. "Ha ha! That's a good one!" He handed the Grinch a flyer, which the Grinch skim-read: "biggest *Who*-ville Christmas ever . . . three times the cheer . . . fun for all *Whos* . . ." Then it was his turn to break into laughter. "Oh, I get it!" the Grinch said. "This is one of your 'joke' things! Finally! Something you said is actually funny!"

Bricklebaum laughed, too. "Yeah, I do joke a lot," he agreed. "But, no, this is actually—"

"Christmas three times bigger!" the Grinch said, still guffawing.

"Look," Bricklebaum said, pointing at the flyer. "It says right there that—"

"It's hysterical!" the Grinch cried, now helpless with laughter. "Oh dear! Ohhhh, no, no, no."

"Well, you're just going to have a good time with this, aren't you?" Bricklebaum observed, chortling. "I have to say, it's really nice to see you laughing."

"Sorry, I can't understand you," the Grinch said, wiping tears

of laughter from under his eyes. "I don't speak ridiculous. Oh, you're a scream. Have a nice life. Goodbye!"

He stomped away through the snow with Max following, pulling the wagon. They headed up the hill towards Mt. Crumpit.

"I'll see you later!" Bricklebaum called after them, waving.

The Grinch and Max continued up the mountain. Partway up, the Grinch dropped Bricklebaum's flyer and stepped on it, trampling it into the snow.

6

That night, Christmas lights came on all over *Who*-ville. Inside Cindy-Lou *Who*'s house, Donna was decorating the tree with the twins, Bean and Buster. Bean moved towards the tree, choosing a good branch for his ornament.

"Yup, that's right," Donna said encouragingly. "That's a great spot. Right there."

But Bean changed course and tried to hang the decoration on Buster's ear instead.

"No, no, not on your brother," Donna said hurriedly. "Let Mummy do it."

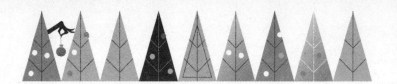

From the top of the stairs, Cindy-Lou looked down at her mum and her brothers through thick snow goggles. She was so bundled up in coats and scarves and gloves and boots, she could barely move. She took one step . . .

. . . and tumbled down the stairs! "Whoa!" she yelled as she rolled down. *THUMP THUMP THUMP THUMP THUMP!*

"Cindy-Lou!" Donna cried, rushing over. "Are you all right?"

"Yeah," Cindy-Lou said, lying there, staring up at the ceiling. "I'm okay."

"You scared me," Donna said.

Cindy-Lou struggled back up on to her feet. "Don't worry, Mum," she said. "I'm wearing four ski jackets. They broke my fall."

"Four jackets?" Donna asked. "Aren't you hot?"

"Yep," Cindy-Lou admitted. "Sweating a little bit."

Donna took a good look at her daughter, dressed for a blizzard, a hurricane and an ice storm all rolled into one. "Are you going somewhere?"

"North Pole," Cindy-Lou answered, pulling a zipper up to her chin.

"Oh, wow!" Donna said. "Any particular reason?"

Cindy-Lou nodded. "I have to talk to Santa."

Donna walked back to the box of Christmas decorations and picked up another one. "Santa, huh?"

"Yeah," her daughter said. "It's really important."

"Well, it must be if you need to go and see him in person," Donna agreed.

Cindy-Lou waddled towards the door. "Yup, it sure is."

"Okay, then," Donna said, hanging the decoration on the tree. "Well, good luck and I'll see you in about a month."

Cindy-Lou stopped in her tracks. "Wait. It takes a whole month to get to the North Pole?"

"Oh yeah," Donna said, reaching in the box for another bauble. "At least."

Cindy-Lou stood by the door, thinking. "Christmas would be over by the time I got there."

"That's true!" Donna said, as though she hadn't thought of it. "Yeah, we would miss you at Christmas."

"Wow," Cindy-Lou said, shaking her head. "I guess I'm going to have to come up with another plan."

Donna hung the bauble on the tree, dug through the box, and pulled out a plastic halo. "Hey, maybe while you're thinking, you could put the halo on the angel," she suggested.

"Okay," Cindy-Lou said.

Donna helped guide her towards the tree. "Do you want to take your jackets off?"

"Yeah, at least one or two of them," Cindy-Lou said, laughing. Donna laughed too and handed the halo to her daughter, looking around for the angel. Then she spotted it.

"No, boys, don't pull the angel's wings off," Donna said, hurrying towards the twins. "She needs those."

At the same moment that Cindy-Lou was deciding not to go to the North Pole to see Santa, the Grinch was standing outside his cave, staring down at *Who*-ville from his chilly perch on Mt. Crumpit. He wasn't decorating a tree that night. And he certainly had no plans to go to see Santa.

He turned away from the twinkling lights of *Who*-ville, went back inside his cave and sat down in his big red chair by the

fireplace. He thought about the *Whos*, all snug in their homes together, and then he thought about himself, sitting all alone.

"It is better this way," he told himself, staring into the crackling fire.

7

At seven the next morning, the Grinch's clock radio turned on and began blaring out from the bottom of the cavern. A jaunty festive tune echoed up into the Grinch's bedroom. He woke up, realised what he was hearing, and gave a loud, frustrated groan. He grabbed a handy chair and hurled it into the cavern, where it smashed down on to the clock radio. At last the radio went silent.

"Heh heh," chuckled the Grinch.

After his morning shower, the Grinch sat hunched over the keyboard of his massive pipe organ, dramatically playing a slow, sad melody. Max did his best to liven up the music on his makeshift

drum kit, with snappy snare hits and cymbal crashes. But every time he played some jaunty rhythms on the drums, the Grinch scowled at him.

As the Grinch came to the end of a particularly gloomy piece of music, Max risked adding a long solo on the cymbals. As he finished with a flourish, the Grinch pointed, ordering Max to leave.

Max slid off his stool and started to go, but not before giving the biggest cymbal one more defiant whack. *CLANG!*

Max lay down in the kitchen and curled up in a sad little ball. Moments later, the Grinch popped through the floor in his mechanical chair. "All right, I'm sorry," the Grinch apologised. "You're a good dog but a bad drummer. What would you like to do?"

Max sat up and wagged his tail. He had an idea!

In the cave's study, which was lined with bookshelves, Max and the Grinch sat in big chairs, playing a game of chess. The Grinch stared down at the board, stuck. He couldn't see a move

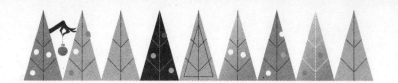

that didn't end with him losing. "More than embarrassing to be beaten by a dog," he muttered to himself. What he needed was a distraction . . .

He grabbed a squeaky ball beneath the table, squeezed it (*SQUEAK SQUEAK*) and then threw it. "Oh, what's that?" he said innocently.

While Max rushed off to investigate, the green cheat quickly rearranged the pieces on the chessboard. "And checkmate!" he announced triumphantly. "Again!"

Suddenly, the whole room started to shake! Pieces fell off the board. Books tumbled from the shelves on to the floor. "What in the world is happening?" the Grinch cried.

He hurried to his front door and flung it open. What could be causing the shaking? An earthquake? Rockslide? Avalanche of snow?

It was none of those things. As he emerged from the cave, the Grinch saw the biggest Christmas tree he'd ever seen, held aloft by several large hot-air balloons. The Grinch's jaw dropped as pine needles rained down on him and Max. "What is that?" the Grinch cried.

"It's the most beautiful Christmas tree in the world!" a familiar voice answered.

The Grinch scowled. Bricklebaum.

He was helping guide the giant tree down the mountain to *Who*-ville, where it would be set up in the town square.

"Three times bigger?" the Grinch said to himself. "That's a hundred times bigger!" he screamed.

"Oh, you just wait until we light it tonight!" Bricklebaum enthused. "It'll sparkle so bright, you'll be celebrating Christmas with the rest of us! Ha ha! Oh, I can't wait! All we have to do is get it safely down the mountain! I'll see you later, Grinchy!"

"No, you will not see me later!" the Grinch called after him. "And I will not be celebrating! And that tree . . . that tree . . . has GOT TO GO!"

The Grinch turned on his heel and went back into his cave, slamming the door behind him. *WHAM!*

That night the streets of *Who*-ville were full of excited *Whos* making their way to the town square for the lighting of the

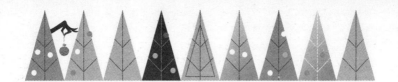

tremendous Christmas tree. They all carried decorations to hang on the tree's branches. It was like a parade!

Cindy-Lou, Donna, Bean and Buster carried the biggest decorations they could find. As they hurried towards the square, they admired their neighbours' colourful baubles in every shape and size.

"Come on, Mum!" Cindy-Lou shouted. She wanted to make sure their angel got a good place on the tree.

Cindy-Lou and her family reached the town square, where Mayor McGerkle was already onstage. "Oh, what a marvellous time of year!" he began. "Welcome, citizens of *Who*-ville, to the annual tree-lighting ceremony! How spectacular are these decorations? Fitting for our spectacular tree!"

Bricklebaum was carrying a huge dragon decoration with a Santa beard and costume. "Look what I made, everybody! It's a Christmas dragon! It came to me in a dream!" Laughing merrily, he lifted the decoration for all to see.

Cindy-Lou handed her family's angel to a *Who* in a crane's bucket that would rise to the top of the tree. "Here you go!"

"Hey, Bartholomew!" Donna said to the *Who*.

"Hey, there, Ms *Who*," he answered cheerfully. "Nice angel!"

"Thank you!" Donna said. "Find a good spot for it!"

Cindy-Lou watched as the bucket rose to the top of the enormous tree. "There it goes," she said. The *Who* carefully placed the angel on the tree.

"Of all the nights in the year," Mayor McGerkle was telling the crowd, "this is my favourite. Now let's get ready to flip that switch and light up the sky!"

The *Whos*, excited and happy, circled the base of the tree.

But up on Mt. Crumpit, watching the ceremony through a large pair of binoculars, the Grinch was not happy. He could tell that the mayor was preparing to flip the switch to turn on the tree's lights. "Oh, no," the Grinch said in a low voice. "Not on my watch, you don't."

8

Down by the tree, Cindy-Lou waved to her mum as she ran off. "See you guys soon! I'm going to go and find Groopert," she said. Groopert was Cindy-Lou's best friend.

"Okay, have fun! Bye!" Donna said. She turned to the twins. "Say 'bye!'" But the boys were too busy staring at all the ornaments to notice.

Groopert was easy to spot with his bright-red curly hair, and Cindy-Lou quickly found him. Today he was running a snowball stand. As Cindy-Lou ran up he handed a snowball to a young

Who. "Here you go," Groopert said. "I hope your big brother gets what he deserves."

"Hey, Groopert!" said Cindy-Lou. "How's business?"

"Good," Groopert said, smiling. "What I can't sell –" he banged his fist on the stand; a board swung down, changing the sign from SNOWBALLS! to SNOWCONES! – "I can always eat!" He poured colourful syrup on a snowball and took a big bite. Then he made a pained face.

"Aw, brain freeze!" he groaned.

"I need to talk to you about something really important," Cindy-Lou told him. "Come on! Let's go!"

"Okay," Groopert said, rubbing his head. He banged his stand again, and a third board swung down with a sign that read, NOW CLOSED! He and Cindy-Lou took off through the crowd.

They knew a good place for important talks. There was a carousel in *Who*-ville with a staircase leading up its central column. The only person who ever used the staircase was the maintenance *Who* in charge of keeping the carousel running smoothly. And,

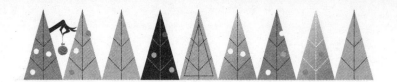

like every other *Who* in *Who*-ville that night, he was at the tree-lighting ceremony.

Cindy-Lou climbed the stairs, her footsteps echoing in the empty chamber. "All right, check this out, Groopert. I'm going to stay up on Christmas Eve this year and meet Santa Claus!"

Groopert was stunned. "Whoa. That is crazy!"

Cindy-Lou turned round to face Groopert. "Yeah," she agreed. "But I've really got to talk to him."

"About what?" Groopert asked as they resumed climbing.

They were almost at the top of the carousel. "Well," she said, "it's really personal, but I'm going to tell you because you're my best friend." They reached the top. From up there, they could see the crowd of *Whos* gathered round the Christmas tree. "It's about my mum," Cindy-Lou continued. "All she ever does is work and take care of us, and it just isn't fair."

Cindy-Lou spotted her mum in the crowd, holding Buster and Bean. "She acts like she's fine," Cindy-Lou said, "but I know it's really hard for her. I figured if anyone could fix that, it'd be Santa."

"Wow," Groopert said, impressed with his friend's generosity. "And I just asked for gum."

Just then, they heard Mayor McGerkle's voice saying, "Here
we go!"

"It's starting!" Cindy-Lou cried.

"My favourite part of the night: the tree lighting!" the mayor
continued. "Okay, *Who*-ville, time to light this beautiful tree!"

But up on Mt. Crumpit, the Grinch had other plans.

He paced along a rocky ledge, counting his steps through the
snow. "Seventeen, eighteen, nineteen and twenty!" Chuckling
darkly, he set the brake on the wheel of a large homemade catapult.
In its bucket sat a huge snowball, which the Grinch intended to
launch right into the *Whos'* Christmas tree!

He hooked a rope to the catapult's lever and walked down
the slope holding the other end. When he yanked the rope, the
catapult would fling the giant snowball at the tree and knock it
over!

"Okay, locked and loaded," the Grinch said gleefully.

Concentrating on the rope, the Grinch didn't notice when the
brake on the catapult's wheel came loose. The catapult started
rolling down the slope, straight towards him.

"ARF! ARF! ARF!" Max warned frantically.

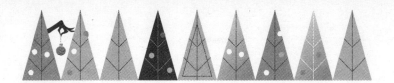

"I know," the Grinch said, not looking up. "I wish I could see the look on their faces when their beloved tree gets—"

WHAM! The catapult slammed into the Grinch, knocking him over the edge of the cliff. The Grinch dangled over the steep drop, holding desperately on to the catapult. "Whoa!" he shouted. "Oh boy, oh boy, oh boy . . ."

The catapult started to tip over the cliff's edge, and the big snowball rolled out of the bucket and right towards him!

"WHOAAAHHH!" He dodged the snowball, which fell harmlessly into the deep ravine.

The Grinch managed to scramble up the main beam of the catapult, where he sat in the bucket and sighed with relief. "Phew! That could have been so much worse—"

SNAP! The rope holding the bucket in place broke! *FWING!* The bucket flew forward! "YAAAAAHHHHH!" The Grinch was flung into the air!

9

Down in the town square, Mayor McGerkle stood near a large light switch at the base of the tree. "Let's begin the countdown!" he called out. "Ready, everyone? Count with me!"

As he spoke the Grinch sailed through the air, rapidly descending from Mt. Crumpit. Like a missile, he headed straight towards the Christmas tree along the path he'd calculated for the giant snowball. "WHOOOOAAAH!" he screamed.

But no one in *Who*-ville heard him. They were too busy counting down to the big moment when the lights would go on. "TEN!" they all shouted together.

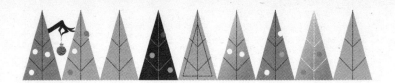

In the sky, The Grinch frantically waved his arms and legs, trying to change his course.

It didn't work.

"NINE!" chanted all the *Whos*.

SCRUNCH! The Grinch flew into the top of the massive tree. "AAUUUGH!" he shrieked as he fell down through the branches and decorations, getting tangled up in tinsel and strings of lights.

"EIGHT! SEVEN! SIX!" the crowd counted down.

The Grinch crashed through the Christmas dragon decoration that Bricklebaum had added to the tree, and ended up wearing it like a costume.

"FIVE!" shouted the crowd.

Dressed as the Christmas dragon and bundled in tinsel, the Grinch flew down the front of the tree.

"FOUR!" the crowd yelled, led by Mayor McGerkle.

"Hey, my dragon can fly!" Bricklebaum said, surprised.

"THREE!" everybody else shouted, including Cindy-Lou and Groopert from the top of the carousel.

The Grinch kept falling, getting closer and closer to the ground. "Oh-no-no-no-no!"

Mayor McGerkle reached for the giant light switch.

"TWO!" chanted all the *Whos*.

The tinsel wrapped round the Grinch reached its full length. As if on cue, his head knocked the light switch on, and then the tinsel yanked him back up into the tree. "Ugghh!" he groaned.

All the *Whos* stared at the huge tree. Thousands of coloured lights twinkled in the crisp night air.

The Grinch dangled near the ground, his foot still caught in the shiny tinsel. "No, no, no!" he protested.

"Aw, the tree's beautiful," Bricklebaum said, his face lighting up in the warm glow of the lights.

Up on the carousel, Cindy-Lou and Groopert gazed at the tree, awestruck by its magnificence.

"Wow," Cindy-Lou said.

"Whoa," Groopert said at the exact same moment.

Mayor McGerkle raised his hand towards it. "There it is!" he said. "The most beautiful tree *Who*-ville has ever seen. Everyone, have a wonderful Christmas season!"

WHUMP! Having finally kicked his foot free of the tinsel, the Grinch fell on to the stage under the tree. On his knees, he looked

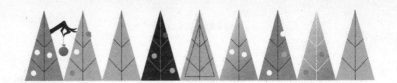

out at the crowd of *Whos*, all celebrating the Christmas season together. His plan had failed and now he was in the very last place he wanted to be. He had to get out!

He slipped into the crowd, moving in the opposite direction from most of the *Whos*, like a fish swimming upstream. "No," he said to himself. "Oh, no, no."

As he struggled through the happy crowd, all the Christmas sights and sounds took him back to his childhood. That was exactly what he'd wanted to avoid. Before he could stop it, the memory of one terrible Christmas long ago came crashing in, as though it were all happening again.

He was just a small boy, standing alone in the Who-ville *orphanage, staring out through the window. He could see all the little* Whos, *the ones with mums and dads, standing around that year's tree, smiling up at the lights and the decorations.*

He walked away from the window and down an empty hallway. He imagined a beautiful tree inside the orphanage, a tree decorated and bright with coloured lights, and surrounded by lots and lots of presents.

Then the vision faded. There was no tree. There were no presents. When it came to the young Grinch, nobody cared.

He looked outside again, and saw young Whos happily running towards their parents. And in that sad, lonely moment, the young Grinch realised that Christmas was the worst day of the year if you were alone.

10

The Grinch tried to make his way through the crowd of *Whos* as quickly as possible, jostled and bumped by all the jolly citizens. Seeing them all so happy made him feel just as wretched as he had when he was a little boy in the *Who*-ville orphanage.

Surrounded by everyone else's joy, the Grinch felt panic growing inside of him. He tried to block the awful memories from flooding his brain, but there was no stopping them now.

He remembered being alone and looking through a window into a *Who* home, seeing the family sit down together at a big dining table to feast on *Who* Pudding and Roast Beast. And then

he remembered standing in the cold winter air, listening as all the *Whos* joined hands round the town Christmas tree and started to sing together.

He knew it would happen again this year on Christmas morning. Everyone in *Who*-ville would gather round the big tree, join hands, open their mouths, and . . .

They'll sing! he thought. *And they'll sing! And they'll SING! SING! SING! SING!*

As he finally broke away from the crowd of merry *Whos*, he said to himself, "I must stop this whole thing!"

He trudged up the twisted path to his cave high on Mt. Crumpit, stomped the snow off his feet, and went in through the front door. Soon he was seated at the bench of his organ, his fingers idly picking out a melancholy tune. He was thinking hard. Max looked on in concern.

"Why, for fifty-three years I've put up with it now!" the Grinch complained. "I must stop this Christmas from coming! But how?"

He played another note on the organ. Max considered joining

in on the drums, but looked at his master's face and thought better of it.

Then the Grinch got an idea! An awful idea! A wonderfully awful idea!

Grinning a terrible grin and snapping his furry fingers, the Grinch announced, "I know just what to do! I'm going to STEAL THEIR CHRISTMAS!"

He rushed upstairs to a window that looked out over *Who-ville* and perched on the sill, delighting in his evil plan. "All the trimmings!" he said. "All the trappings! All their gifts and garlands!"

Max, who had followed him up to the window, stared at the Grinch with his eyes open wide.

"When they wake and see it's gone," the Grinch told his dog, "then all their joy and happiness will be gone as well! So prepare yourself, Max! For tomorrow . . . we begin!"

Very early the next morning, Max was sleeping on his little mattress when—*DING-A-LING-A-LING!* The bell rang! The Grinch was already awake!

Max quickly made his master's coffee, set it on the tray, balanced the tray on his head and backed into the mini-lift. But as it neared the Grinch's bedroom, Max heard an unfamiliar sound – something moving on the floor above him.

DING! The mini-lift reached the bedroom and the door opened. When Max stepped out, he got another surprise.

The Grinch, dressed in workout clothes, was already up and exercising! He bent and stretched, chanting, "And squat and up, and squat and up, and squat!" He looked at Max through his legs. "Genius starts with the abs, Max!" he said.

After a few more squats and bends, the Grinch stood up straight and squared his shoulders. At last he said, "It's go time."

The Grinch and Max sat in the red chair. This time, instead of rising into the dining room, it took off, shooting down through a tunnel to the Grinch's basement workshop. The stony chamber was full of all kinds of gizmos, gadgets and unfinished inventions. The Grinch hopped out of the chair, put Max down and strode over to a gigantic blackboard.

"And now the question we have all been asking ourselves," he said, tapping the blackboard with his fingers. "*How* will I steal

Christmas? Well, Max, prepare to have your little doggy mind blown!"

"ARF!" Max barked, eagerly wagging his tail.

With a grand flourish, the Grinch flipped the giant blackboard round to reveal what he'd written on the other side in the middle of the night. Max expected to see an elaborate plan ... but the blackboard contained only two words, in small spindly writing: Sanᴛa Claus.

"Ta-da!" the Grinch said proudly.

Max raised an eyebrow. "Arf?"

"You see, I will become Santa Claus!" the Grinch explained. "But instead of giving all the joy and happiness, I'll take it away! If he can deliver Christmas to the whole world in one night, then I can certainly steal it from little old *Who*-ville. I mean, come on! What does Santa have that I don't?"

Max barked. "ARF!"

The Grinch frowned as he considered what Max had said, and then pointed a finger at him and replied, "That's hurtful."

11

W hile the Grinch was explaining his dastardly scheme to Max, Donna *Who* was in her kitchen, a fork in each hand, trying to get Buster and Bean to eat waffles. The twins stubbornly kept their mouths tightly shut and their arms folded across their chests.

"Choo choo!" Donna said, trying to make her best train sounds. "Okay, make a tunnel! Here comes the waffle train! Open up, here it comes! Choo choo!"

RUMBLE. A bowling ball rolled through the door and across the kitchen floor. Donna stared at it as Cindy-Lou ran after it.

"What are you doing with my bowling ball?" Donna asked.

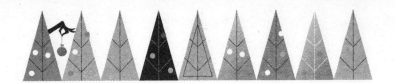

"Chasing it," Cindy-Lou answered as she crossed the kitchen and scooped up the heavy ball.

"And you're taking it where?" Donna asked.

"It's a secret," Cindy-Lou said as she headed for the door.

"All right," Donna replied. "But not without breakfast! Catch!" She snatched a couple of waffles off a plate and tossed them across the kitchen to Cindy-Lou, who caught them and stuffed them into her bag.

"Waffles!" Cindy-Lou said happily. "My favourite! Thanks! See you guys later!"

Outside, the sun was up, glinting and sparkling off the clean white snow. Cindy-Lou stowed the bowling ball in her snow-bike and jumped on.

She took off through the streets of *Who*-ville, sliding along the slick snow and ice. When she reached Groopert's house, she parked next to a tree, cupped her hands to her mouth and called out, "Ka-kaw! Ka-kaw!"

A bag flew down and landed in the shiny, egg-shaped sidecar on Cindy-Lou's snow-bike. Then Groopert stuck his head out of a window of the house's second floor. He'd heard Cindy-Lou's

"Ka-kaw" (their pre-arranged secret signal) and answered it with his own "Woop woop!" He made sure the coast was clear before pulling out a textbook, opening it and draping it over a branch of the tree just outside his window. Holding on to the covers of the book, he slid down the bending branch like he was riding a zip line before dropping into the sidecar.

"Ready!" he said.

"All right," Cindy-Lou said, grinning. "Let's go!"

She stood up on the pedals and they took off, sliding through the streets and out of *Who*-ville. They went into the forest on the edge of town, following a path they knew well.

"Hold on!" Cindy-Lou warned, as they rode on to the end of a large log.

"Whoo!" they both whooped as their weight tipped the other end of the log down, depositing them on the next part of their secret pathway. Eventually they reached a huge tree with an elaborate fort tucked in its branches.

"Let's go! Let's go! Let's move!" Groopert said excitedly, as they climbed out of the snow-bike.

Two ends of a long, sturdy rope hung down from the tree fort. One

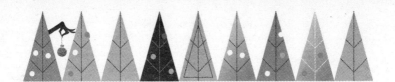

end had a large, upside-down-T-shaped bar tied to it; the other a bag. Groopert dropped the bowling ball into the bag, and he and Cindy-Lou climbed on to the T-bar, standing on either side and holding on to the rope. Groopert let the bag with the bowling ball drop.

"Hang on!" Groopert called out as the weight of the bowling ball pulled the rope and the T-bar up to the tree fort. They sailed high up the trunk. "Wooooooo!" When they reached the top, he said, "And dismount!" The two friends jumped on to the wooden floor of the tree fort.

Cindy-Lou dug the waffles out of her backpack, put them on a plate, and poured syrup on them. As Groopert sat and ate the waffles, Cindy-Lou flipped over a sheet of paper on an easel. She found a marker and wrote, Santa Claus. Then she tapped the paper with her marker.

"So," she said. "What do we know?"

"Waff-ulz er de-wicious," Groopert said with his mouth full.

"Super delicious," Cindy-Lou agreed, "but I meant about meeting Santa Claus."

Groopert thought a moment, chewing. He swallowed and said, "We know no one's ever done it."

"Hmmm," Cindy-Lou said, thinking. "Okay, how about this? On Christmas Eve night, I'm going to sit in our living room with my eyes wide open,"

She opened her eyes as wide as they'd go. Staring at Groopert, she looked a little like a startled owl.

"And if I start to drift off to sleep, I'll just open my eyes wider."

"Um, I'm pretty sure you're going to fall asleep anyway," Groopert objected. "And by the time you wake up—"

"He'll be gone," Cindy-Lou admitted. She knew it was true.

"Poof!" Groopert said, moving his hands like a magician revealing a missing bunny. "Nothing but cookie crumbs!"

Cindy-Lou nodded.

They sat there in silence for a moment, thinking.

Then Groopert sat up straight. "I've got it!"

"Tell me!" Cindy-Lou said eagerly.

"Maple syrup!" Groopert said.

"All right," Cindy-Lou said slowly, not knowing where he was going with this. "Maple syrup . . . ?"

"We pour it on the roof," Groopert explained. "The reindeer

get stuck. And then they can't fly away. Science." He folded his arms and smiled a satisfied smile.

Cindy-Lou wasn't so sure. "Won't the syrup just freeze?"

"Good point," Groopert agreed, his smile fading.

Then something dawned on her. "Wait a minute!" she cried. "I THINK I'VE GOT IT!" Excited, Cindy-Lou headed out of the tree fort.

"Where are you going?" Groopert asked.

"We're going to need the whole gang for this one," Cindy-Lou replied.

"Okay," said Groopert. "Just let me finish my waffles."

12

The Grinch was back in his study with Max. But this time they weren't playing chess. The Grinch ran his finger along the books on the shelves, scanning the titles, searching for a particular volume. "Aha!" he finally exclaimed, pulling a thick book down from the top shelf. *"Cringle's Christmas Almanac!"* He stopped a moment to think. "Why do I own this?" Then he remembered. "Ah, yes. Bricklebaum," the Grinch said. "He gave it to me. *Typical.*"

The Grinch crossed over to his desk with the big volume tucked under his arm. "Okay," he said, opening it. "If I'm going to become Santa, then I need to get into character."

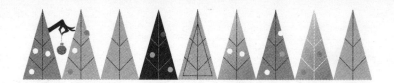

He started flipping through the pages. "All right, let's see. Christmas tree, Christmas traditions, Christmas pudding . . ."

From his spot on the floor, Max watched his master curiously.

"Where is the Santa stuff?" said the Grinch, frustrated. As he continued to turn the pages, he happened upon a picture of a family at Christmas. "Oh my goodness, look at this," he scoffed. "Little girls and boys giggling over sugarplums."

The Grinch found himself being drawn into the heart-warming illustration despite himself. "Oooh, look at how they did the roof of the gingerbread house with vanilla icing," he said. "And made a little family of gumdrops!" But then he caught himself, and went back into his usual sour mode. "So dumb. So, so stupidly dumb."

Finally, the Grinch found what he was looking for. "Ah! Here we are!" he exclaimed. "The Legend of Santa Claus!" He scanned the page. "Red suit, white beard, always in a jolly mood."

"Oh . . ." He looked up at Max. "Well, that's not going to happen."

The Grinch slammed the book closed, pushed his chair back, and stood up. "Oh, well. Let's just start with a sleigh and go find ourselves some reindeer."

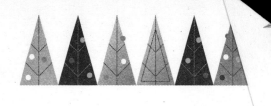

After putting on warm scarves, the Grinc̶͟ ͟ᵤd
outside and down the mountain. They hiked ͦ͟ugh the forest
until they reached an outcropping of stone that overlooked the
meadows below.

The Grinch pulled out a horn decorated with elaborate
carvings. "Beautiful, isn't it?" he said, showing the horn to Max.
"This, my little friend, is the rein-horn. It perfectly recreates the
call of the reindeer. Observe!"

He held the horn up to his lips, took a deep breath, and blew.
BAAAAAAAAH!

The Grinch lowered the horn and waited for reindeer to
come running. But none did. Then after a moment, a lone goat
wandered up.

"Oh," said the Grinch. "Hey there. Sorry, little goat, I was
calling for a rein—"

"BAAAAAAAAH!" The goat screamed a tremendously loud
scream.

"Aaaah!" yelled the Grinch. "What was that?" He tried
to shoo the goat away with his hands. "Scram! Skedaddle, you
strange goat!"

But the goat just stared. The Grinch and Max decided to find a new spot to call the reindeer.

Soon they'd found a promising place. Stopping to look around, the Grinch told Max, "Now, reindeer migrate, so maybe we'll catch a few headed south for the winter. I also read they tend to bed down for the night in—"

He whirled around and, without taking a breath, addressed the goat that was following them through the wilderness, "Will you stop following us? Shoo! Away! Go back to the goat farm! Go eat a can!"

The Grinch and Max pressed on. "Ugh," the Grinch said. "Now that that's over, back to the task at hand. Ooo! It's a little crisp!"

It was more than crisp. As the Grinch and Max trudged along, the temperature plummeted, and a blizzard began to howl. "It's g-g-getting really c-c-cold!" the Grinch observed, his teeth chattering. "Can't feel my lips! Can't . . . blink . . . Eyes frozen."

By the time they reached the peak of a mountain, the Grinch was nearly frozen solid, and Max was partially encased in a cube of ice! But when they looked down through their icicle-fringed eyes, they saw a huge herd of reindeer in the valley below!

"Max!" the Grinch managed to say. "We've hit the mother lode! We'll have a hundred reindeer to pull our—"

"*BAAAAAAAAAAHHHHH!*" The screaming goat reappeared just in time to give one last ear-piercing scream, loud enough to blast Max and the Grinch out of their icy casing!

They watched disbelievingly as, at the sound of the goat's scream, all the reindeer below stampeded away.

The Grinch stood still, the sound of the goat's scream ringing in his ears. But then, as the mist cleared in the valley below, he saw that there remained . . . a single, very hairy, and somewhat overweight, reindeer.

He and Max made their way down into the valley, slowly approaching the big reindeer. They stopped behind a tree and peered round to look. "Well, Santa had eight," he said to Max with a sigh. "This one looks like he ate the other seven." He went into a stealthy crouch. "Watch and learn, Max," he whispered.

The Grinch tunnelled down into the snow, then popped up behind the chubby reindeer, a lasso raised in one hand. The reindeer stood still, slowly chewing on grass. *All right,* thought the Grinch. *Now to toss this lasso round your—*

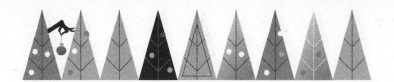

But just as he was about to throw his rope, the reindeer moved, shuffling to a different spot to find more grass under the snow.

The Grinch followed, taking up a new position behind him. "Heh heh heh," he chuckled softly as he swung his lasso. He let it fly . . . but it missed its target, and instead landed on the reindeer's back. The reindeer looked up from his grazing, and the Grinch dove to hide himself beneath the snow.

But the tuft of green hair on the top of his head stuck out amid the dazzling whiteness.

The reindeer ambled over to the tuft. How had he missed this delicious patch of grass? The reindeer licked its lips.

CHOMP!

"AHHH!" the Grinch screamed, bursting up out of the snow and holding his new bald spot.

Terrified, the reindeer took off running, but the Grinch managed to hurl his lasso round the animal's neck as it fled. *TWANG!* The rope pulled tight, and the Grinch was yanked off his feet. He went flying after the reindeer, bumping over mounds of snow. "AAAAAHHHHHHGH!"

The Grinch managed to get his feet on the ground and stand

up for a second, skiing over the snow. "Ha ha!" he laughed triumphantly. But seconds later—

WHAM! The Grinch slammed right into the thick trunk of a tree!

The next thing he knew, he was lying on his back in the snow, being licked by a big, wet reindeer tongue.

13

As the sun set, the Grinch, Max and the chubby reindeer walked across a snowy field, making their way home.

"Keep walking," the Grinch told his two companions. "We are headed towards destiny."

Back in *Who*-ville, Cindy-Lou had summoned the rest of her gang to meet in the town's maze of Christmas lights. Cindy-Lou and Groopert had arrived first and were eagerly awaiting the others' arrival.

When she saw her friends Ozzy, Izzy and Axl walking up, Cindy-Lou grinned. Axl, wearing a blue coat and a striped scarf,

was the tallest. Ozzy was much shorter, with goggles strapped around his winter hat. Shortest of all was Izzy. She wore big, round black glasses, a scarf and earmuffs.

"All right," Ozzy said. "You called, we came."

"So, what's up?" Izzy asked.

"Yeah, what's the deal?" Axl asked.

"Thanks for getting here so fast, guys," Cindy-Lou said. "Follow me."

She took off through the maze, followed by Izzy, Ozzy, Axl and Groopert.

"So, what's the big secret?" Axl asked as they trotted along.

"Yeah, I don't have very long," Ozzy said. "My parents set the timer."

"Dude," Axl said.

Ozzy knew what his friend meant. Something along the lines of, *You're telling me your parents actually set a timer, and you have to be back home before the timer goes off or you'll be in trouble? Dude* could mean a lot.

"Don't ask," Ozzy said, shaking his head. "It's new."

Cindy-Lou led the gang down narrow paths between high

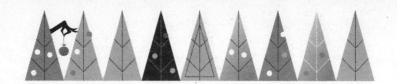

walls lit by thousands of coloured lights. Other children chased each other through the maze, laughing and screaming.

The five friends passed through a tall curtain of lights into the centre of the maze, which was complete with a giant illuminated Santa Claus.

"All right, everybody," Cindy-Lou said, "brace yourselves. In exactly forty-eight hours, we are going to do something that's never been done before." She took a deep breath. "We're going to trap Santa Claus."

The others looked stunned. Ozzy broke the silence. "Trap Santa? Why would we want to do that?"

"Duh, to steal all the toys!" Axl said. "I love it."

Ozzy and Izzy had to agree that sounded like a great idea!

"No," Cindy-Lou said quickly. "Not to steal the toys. To, um, talk to him."

"What?" Ozzy said, confused. "Why would you want to talk to him?"

"It's personal," Groopert explained.

"Yeah, it's kind of personal," Cindy-Lou confirmed.

"Well, I don't want to do it if you won't tell me why," insisted Ozzy stubbornly.

"What are you talking about, 'personal'?" Axl asked.

Cindy-Lou turned to him. "Axl, when you asked to borrow sixteen dollars and my mum's suitcase, did I ask you why?"

Axl thought about it. "No," he admitted.

She turned to Ozzy. "And what about you, Ozzy? Remember when you got stuck in that—"

"All right, all right, okay, geez," Ozzy said quickly, cutting her off. He didn't want that particular embarrassing incident brought up again.

"I did it because you're my friends," Cindy-Lou continued. "And when something matters to you, that means it matters to me."

They all stood there a moment. Then Groopert said, "That's beautiful."

"Okay, okay, okay," Axl grumbled. "You convinced me."

"Count me in, too," Ozzy said.

"All right, we're in," Izzy added.

Cindy-Lou grinned. "Great! Now let's do this! To the bikes!"

Moments later, the five friends were on their snow-bikes, breezing down the slick streets of *Who*-ville. But they hadn't gotten far when they heard their parents calling. "Let's go – dinnertime!" "Cindy-Lou, dinnertime!" "Time to eat!"

"Ooo!" Groopert said, licking his lips. "Dinner!"

They hit the brakes and came to a stop in the middle of the street. "All right," Cindy-Lou said. "We meet first thing in the morning."

"Okay," Groopert said.

"All right, see you tomorrow," Ozzy agreed.

"See you all in the morning," Axl said.

"OZZY! TIMER!" Ozzy's mother bellowed.

"Okay, Mum!" Ozzy called off, hurrying towards home. He had no interest in finding out what happened when the timer actually went off.

14

The Grinch had a reindeer. (He'd decided to call him Fred.) Now he needed a sleigh.

And he knew just where to get one.

That night, the Grinch and Max snuck through Bricklebaum's garden, hiding behind what appeared to be a big mound of snow. The mound of snow shifted – it was Fred in disguise!

The Grinch crept through the garden as quietly as possible, placing his feet down gingerly. But with every step, the snow made a loud *CRUNCH*. "This is the loudest snow I've ever heard in my life," he muttered.

When they got close to the house, all lit up with Christmas lights, the Grinch pointed to the roof. "See up there?" he asked Max and Fred. "That's our sleigh."

Max and Fred both looked up at the huge sleigh on top of Bricklebaum's roof. They shared a doubtful look. How were they going to get it off the roof without anyone noticing?

"You two go round the back," the Grinch instructed them. "Wait for me to drop the sleigh from the roof. Okay – go, team!"

As Max and Fred headed round to the back of Bricklebaum's house, the Grinch tiptoe-crunched through the snow towards a ladder that Bricklebaum had left outside. But as the Grinch passed the house, he saw Bricklebaum's dog, Mabel, sleeping on the other side of a doggy door. She was round and grey, with a pink bow in her fur. "Oh!" the Grinch said to himself softly. "Shhh!"

He carefully picked up the ladder and leaned it against the house, keeping an eye on the sleeping dog. But as he stepped on to the first rung, the ladder sank straight into the snow under his weight. "No!" he cried in frustration, before he could stop himself. "No, no, no!"

That woke Mabel. She looked out and saw the Grinch. He laughed nervously.

Mabel came tearing out through the doggy door and started nipping at the Grinch's heels. "Ow!" he yelped. "Ahh!"

The Grinch pulled himself up on to a balcony to escape, and Mabel ran back into the house. "Phew!" the Grinch said, stopping to catch his breath. But then Mabel's head appeared out of a window by the balcony, looking for the intruder. "Ahh!" the Grinch yelled.

Mabel hopped out of the window, chasing the Grinch. He ran from her and slipped. He kicked his feet in panic, accidentally pressing the doorbell with his toe. *DING-DONG!*

Down below, Mabel barked up at him. "RARF! RARF!"

WHOMP! A big pile of snow fell off the roof and on to Mabel, momentarily burying her. As the Grinch clung to the gutter, Bricklebaum came out to see who had rung his doorbell. "Who's there?" he asked into the darkness. "What's going on?"

The Grinch's fingers were giving out one by one, and he was about to fall when Mabel popped up out of the snow in front of Bricklebaum.

"Hey, who taught Mabel how to use the doorbell?" Bricklebaum asked. "Man, that's awesome! You smart little dog!" He scooped Mabel up, kissed the top of her head and carried her back into the warm house.

Straining and grunting, the Grinch managed to pull himself up and continue his climb towards the roof. As he passed a window, he paused to look inside. "Eh, what's this?"

Bricklebaum and his party guests were earnestly singing a classic Christmas song. The Grinch stared at them through the window for a moment. Part of him longed to be inside with them. But then he shook his head and continued climbing.

Through another window, Mabel spotted the Grinch again. Growling, she raced out of the room to find the intruder. Bricklebaum didn't notice her go, as he was busy picking the next song for his guests to sing.

Moments later, the Grinch finally pulled himself on to the roof. He crossed to the sleigh and looked down at Max and Fred waiting in the back garden. "All right!" he hissed to them. "Here it comes! Get ready! Easy as taking candy from a baby."

Holding on to the chimney, he bent down to unhook the

cords tying the sleigh to the roof . . . and saw Mabel, teeth bared, snarling. "Grrrrr—"

"Uh," the Grinch said, "good puppy?"

Mabel launched herself at the Grinch. He let go of the chimney and slid down the roof. With the sleigh's cords unhooked, it fell, hitting a balcony on its way down.

The Grinch swung into Bricklebaum's house through a window at the end of the party room, with Mabel in his arms growling and snapping. No one saw him as he tossed Mabel aside. The little dog sailed past party guests, snagging their cocoa and cake. She stopped on a table, right in front of Bricklebaum.

"Look at that!" Bricklebaum exclaimed, laughing. "Mabel is delivering cakes now! I mean, is this the best Christmas ever, or what?"

Outside, the sleigh had fallen to the ground. The Grinch plunged back out of the window, landing in the seat next to Max. Fred took off, pulling the sleigh behind him.

Through the window, Bricklebaum caught a glimpse of the sleigh gliding away in the distance. "Wow!" he said. "I think I just saw Santa Claus!"

15

B ack in his cave, the Grinch got ready for bed with a spring
in his step. "Today was great!" he announced. "We did mean
things and we did them in style!"

As he climbed into bed, he looked down at the floor and saw
Max staring up at him. "Max, don't do puppy eyes," he scolded.
"You know the rules. You sleep in your bed, and I sleep in—"

As he turned away, he found himself face to face with Fred.
"WHAA!" the Grinch shouted. "Fred! Okay, please tell me you're
joking. No! No, no!"

Fred tried to climb on to the bed. The Grinch tried to push

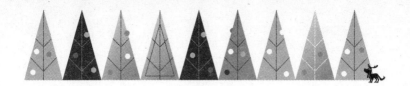

him away, but Fred was big and heavy. And he *really* wanted to get into the bed. After some wrestling, the Grinch succeeded in shoving Fred back to the floor.

Fred stared at him with sad eyes from one side of the bed.

And Max did the same from the other.

"Oh, no, no," the Grinch said. "Not you too. I don't believe this. Max, did you teach Fred puppy eyes?"

They both kept staring at him with their big, sad eyes.

"Fine," the Grinch relented with a sigh. "This one time."

Max and Fred hopped into the Grinch's bed, making the springs squeal in protest. Though it was crowded, they all got comfortable and settled down to sleep. Soon, the Grinch was snoring. No one, much less the Grinch himself, would have guessed it, but there was a tiny smile on his face.

The next morning, Fred walked into the kitchen. He spotted the complicated coffee machine.

When Max headed in to make the Grinch's coffee a short while later, he found Fred balanced on the machine, trying to make a

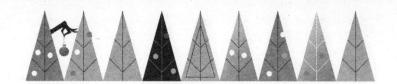

cup himself! The chubby reindeer stepped on the plunger, and the coffee gushed into the cup.

Fred smiled and Max sighed in relief.

A little later, the Grinch, Fred and Max sat at the dining-room table eating breakfast. "Mmm," the Grinch said appreciatively. "Now THAT is a great cup of coffee!"

Fred smiled again. Max narrowed his eyes as if to say, "Making coffee is MY job!"

"Max," the Grinch said to his faithful pup, "this morning you and I need to gather some information. Fred, you just sit right there . . . and don't touch anything!"

After they'd finished breakfast, the Grinch and Max headed to the cliff just outside the cave's front door. Max wore a harness with several propellers, a cluster of cameras on his head and a doubtful expression on his face.

The Grinch stood next to a monitor wearing a headset microphone. "Okay, Max," he said calmly. "I'll be in your ear the whole time and, whatever you're seeing, I'll be seeing on the monitor. Ready?"

Max was still unsure about the whole thing. Paying no

attention, the Grinch pressed a button on his remote control. The propellers started to spin. "Now off you go, Max!" the Grinch said. "Fly, boy! Fly!"

Toggling the switches on the controller, the Grinch sent Max soaring off towards *Who*-ville. "If we are going to steal Christmas, we need to know as much about *Who*-ville as possible," said the Grinch through Max's earpiece. How many houses are in *Who*-ville? How many *Whos*? How many wreaths and trees? How many chimneys?"

Flying between two birds, Max waved at one of them. The bird just looked confused.

Thanks to the camera, the Grinch could see exactly what Max was looking at. "Max," he chided. "Stop socialising. Now, let's go in for a look."

Max swooped in over the houses of *Who*-ville. "Okay," the Grinch said. "Twelve houses on Elm Street. That means—Oh! Watch out!"

Max had come too close to a *Who* in the bucket of a crane who was putting up Christmas decorations. "Huh?" said the *Who*. "What was that?"

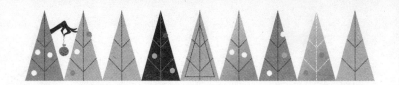

Max quickly flew round a corner, out of the *Who*'s sight. The man shrugged and went back to his work, humming a festive tune.

"Okay," the Grinch said to Max through the headset. "Go, go, go!"

Emerging from his hiding place, Max flew down the street. "Now cut through Main Street," the Grinch ordered, "and survey the south side."

Max swooped down Main Street, flying above all the *Who* shoppers going about their business with no idea what was happening above their heads.

"Look at those greedy little gift monsters loading themselves up with Christmas junk," the Grinch sneered. "It's all they care about."

When Max reached the end of the street, the Grinch said, "Okay, turn right here!"

As Max buzzed over the pavement, Bricklebaum passed below him. He was telling a friend, "So I woke up this morning, got dressed, had my coffee, went outside, looked on the roof and my sleigh was gone! A mystery!"

Listening on his headset, the Grinch grinned. "My, my. I wonder who took it!"

Suddenly, Max spotted something very interesting in front of one of the shops . . . He steered himself towards it. The Grinch was busy calculating: "If we do twenty-eight houses an hour for six hours that would be . . . sausages?"

His monitor was filled with strings of sausages getting closer and closer. Max was clearly flying straight for them. "No," the Grinch barked. "Don't even think about it!"

But Max couldn't resist the delicious sausages. As he flew by, he craned his neck round and bit the nearest one. The whole string of sausages came loose, getting caught in Max's propellers. His flying gizmo wobbled out of control!

"MAAAAAXXX!" the Grinch yelled.

Max swooped and dipped and whipped around the sky above *Who*-ville!

The Grinch stared at the monitor, trying to figure out where Max was. "Max?"

He saw something green and furry on the monitor – small at first, but getting bigger and bigger. It looked just like . . . "Oh, hey, look! It's me!" the Grinch cried. "AHHHH!"

He turned round and Max walloped right into him – *WHAM!*

16

After the Grinch had picked himself up, he and Max went back inside the cave. "Mission accomplished!" the Grinch sang out. "Fred!"

There was no answer. The Grinch and Max headed into the kitchen. It was a complete mess! "Fred! What are you doing?" the Grinch cried.

Fred looked at them. He was sucking on the nozzle of a can of whipped cream. Cream shot out of his nose and he sniffed it back in.

The Grinch sighed. "Come on. We've got work to do."

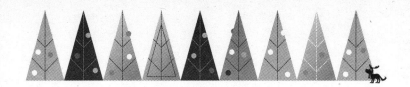

The Grinch had converted one of the cave's bigger chambers into a command centre for Operation Steal Christmas, complete with a detailed model of *Who*-ville. He stuck a ball of red wool onto Fred's antler. "Now let's plan our route," the Grinch said.

He grabbed the end of the red wool and pulled, using it along with some tacks to lay down a route through the model town. The ball spun quickly, letting out more wool as the Grinch raced around the model. "First, we go south. Then a quick jaunt to the east. And then this house – skip the subdivision for the moment – knock off the entire southeast quadrant, and –" the Grinch stuck his last tack in the model version of Cindy-Lou *Who*'s house – "then we finish it all up on Whistling-*Who* Lane. That's two hundred and twenty-three houses and only seven hours of darkness to work with. That means we have to be FAST and FOCUSED!"

The Grinch paced back and forth in front of Max and Fred like a general addressing his troops. "There will be temptation all around us!" he barked.

He pressed a button. A curtain opened, revealing a gorgeous,

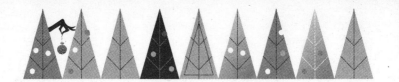

elaborate mock-up of a living room decorated for Christmas, including a tree with lots of presents under it.

"Behold," the Grinch said, "the present!" He grabbed a wrapped gift from under the tree. He looked at the shining box with great distrust. "This is our enemy. You will want to unwrap it and play with it. You'll think it would be fun. Lots of fun . . ." For a moment, it looked as though the Grinch himself was thinking about doing those very things. But he regained his steely composure. "But you must not! And after you get past the present, a challenging obstacle still remains . . ."

He held up a biscuit shaped like a Christmas tree and covered in red icing and sprinkles. It looked absolutely scrumptious. "The biscuit! Look at it in all its red sugary splendour . . ."

Staring, Max and Fred moved towards the biscuit with their tongues hanging out.

"No, no, no!" the Grinch warned, shaking his head.

Max and Fred were still staring and drooling.

"Discipline!" the Grinch snapped. "We must—"

CHOMP!

Fred ate the whole biscuit in one big bite.

"Resist," the Grinch concluded, sighing.

In Cindy-Lou's house, the gang had gathered in the living room. Cindy-Lou knelt in front of the fireplace. "Are you ready?" she called up into the darkness.

"Almost," came Groopert's voice down the chimney.

"Good," Cindy-Lou said. "Think jolly."

"And fat!" Ozzy added.

There was a moment of silence.

"Okay," Groopert called down. "I'm ready."

Cindy-Lou turned to Ozzy, Izzy and Axl. "All right, quick! Everybody hide!"

The four friends ran behind the sofa. "Three, two, one, cue Santa!" Cindy-Lou yelled.

Nothing happened.

"That means you, Groopert," Cindy-Lou explained.

"WAAAAH!" Groopert yelled, tumbling down the chimney. *CLUNK!* He hit the bottom and rolled out of the fireplace into the living room. He was dressed as Santa, and looked a little blackened and battered from his trip down the chimney.

Groopert stood up and looked around. Speaking in his best

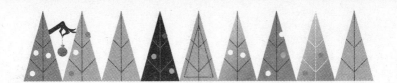

Santa voice, he said, "Ho, ho, ho, ho! Look at this pretty house! I will leave presents for the people!"

"Come on," Ozzy said, reacting to Groopert's line delivery. "It's not the school play, dude."

"Then why do I have to wear the outfit?" Groopert asked, not unreasonably.

"Groopert, focus!" Cindy-Lou said. "Just get the cookie."

Groopert looked across the room. He saw a chocolate-chip cookie sitting inside a white-chalk circle next to a sign that read, FOR SANTA. He walked over to it. He reached towards the cookie, then hesitated. "But I can see the string," he objected.

"Stop worrying," Izzy said. "It'll be dark at night."

"What if he has a torch?" Groopert asked.

Cindy-Lou made a face. "Have you ever seen a picture of Santa with a torch?"

"No," Groopert admitted, "but I think he might—"

"Groopert," Cindy-Lou said firmly. "Just pick up the cookie!"

Groopert went back to his Santa voice. "Ho, ho, ho, what do we have here? A delicious little cookie!" He grabbed it and – *SWOOP!* – a rope yanked him out of the room. "AHHHH!" he screamed.

The other kids saw Groopert fly out of the window. They ran to it and looked out. "Groopert!" Cindy-Lou called.

But instead of Groopert, only his clothes were hanging from the branch of a tree. "Groopert?" Cindy-Lou repeated, confused.

"Uh, hey, guys?" a voice said from behind them. They whipped round and saw Groopert standing in front of the fireplace in his underwear. He was holding the cookie. "Do I still get to eat this?"

17

Up on Mt. Crumpit, the Grinch stood with Max and Fred next to something big covered by a tarpaulin. "All right," he said proudly. "So, I tinkered with our sleigh a bit. Behold!"

He whipped off the tarp, revealing Bricklebaum's sleigh, to which the Grinch had added a miniature sidecar. "Look at this, Max! You'll be riding in style. A throne for a barking prince! How do you like that?"

Wagging his tail happily, Max jumped into the sidecar.

The Grinch led Fred to the sleigh's harness. "Fred, you are the engine of this great machine. Understood?"

Fred's face remained blank.

"Good," said the Grinch.

Fred stepped into the harness. The Grinch gave his two assistants a quick pep talk. "Now remember: this is just a practice run. But in this team we practise like we play! So, let's leave it all out on the snow!"

Max barked his agreement. The Grinch climbed into the sleigh and took up the reins. He pressed a button, and a segmented mechanical arm shot out and grabbed Fred's tail. *ZHWOOM!* They took off across the snow!

"Oooooh!" the Grinch whooped. "All right!"

Moving at a casual clip, Fred pulled the sleigh along a mountain path – up, down, and around a bend.

"Now let's pick up the pace and see how it handles!" the Grinch said, shaking the reins.

"ARF! ARF!" Max barked as Fred broke into a gallop.

"Whooooooah!" the Grinch shouted.

Fred ran even faster, taking curves like a champ. He was beginning to enjoy himself. But as the sleigh rounded the edge of another cliff, it tipped dangerously.

"Whoa, hold on!" the Grinch shouted.

Fred skittered across a frozen pond and wove between trees, going faster and faster!

"Ha ha!" the Grinch laughed. "We're doing it, Max! We are doing it! We will not be—"

SCREECH! Fred came to a sudden halt. The Grinch slammed into the front of the sleigh. WHAM!

"What happened?" the Grinch asked. "Fred?"

Then he saw two reindeer walking towards them, an adult female and a baby. "Sorry," the Grinch told them, "we don't need any more reindeer."

But the two reindeer kept coming.

"No!" the Grinch shouted, flicking his hands at them. "Go! Get! Shoo! I have what I need!"

Behind him, the Grinch heard a loud reindeer call, full of joy. He turned and saw Fred with his chin lifted and his mouth wide open, bugling. An answering call came from the female deer. The Grinch looked confused. But then the two reindeer walked right up to Fred, and all three lovingly nuzzled each other. For a moment, the Grinch felt warm and fuzzy inside seeing them together. Finally, he understood.

This was Fred's family.

"It's okay, Fred," the Grinch said with a sigh. He undid the harness, and Fred walked away with his family. The Grinch watched them go.

"On our own again, Max," he said. Max wagged his tail. The Grinch couldn't help but smile back.

18

The next morning, on the day before Christmas, lots of *Whos* were happily finishing up their last-minute shopping in central *Who*-ville. Carolers sang Christmas carols, and *Who* families, including Cindy-Lou's, had their Christmas portraits taken.

"All right," Donna said as they posed for the photographer. "Everyone ready?"

They all smiled. *FLASH!* As the camera clicked, Bean leaped for a passing candy cane, Donna leaped for him and Buster inserted his finger up Cindy-Lou's nose. Another picture-perfect moment was captured.

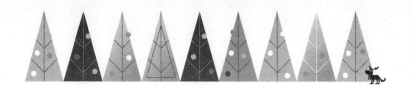

The forecast was for more snow – wonderful Christmas weather. It looked as though this was going to be the best Christmas of all!

Up on Mt. Crumpit, the Grinch was putting the finishing touches to his nasty plan.

DING-A-LING! The bell woke Max bright and early. He cocked his head, listening carefully. The ringing wasn't coming from the Grinch's bedroom. It was coming from the workshop.

Max made the Grinch's coffee, balanced the tray on his head as usual and hurried through the stony halls to the workshop. When he pushed the door open, he saw the Grinch, looking a bit frazzled and wild-eyed, as though he'd been up all night – which he had.

"Max!" the Grinch cried. "There you are! Check this out!" He held up his furry feet. He was wearing extendo-shoes, which lowered as he walked towards Max. It was as though the Grinch had automatic ladders built into his shoes to lift and lower him. "I have been up all night making stuff to help us with our magnificent plan! Oooo . . . more coffee!"

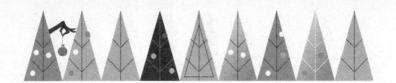

He eagerly lifted the cup off the tray on Max's head. "It's going to be a big night," he said. "Very exciting! And speaking of exciting, I've got some great news for you. Come with me!"

He scooped Max up in his arms and carried him outside. Then the Grinch plopped his dog down in front of the sleigh. "Max, do you know what you are? You are a sturdy little fella. And loyal. Very loyal. In fact, I think you're the best dog a Grinch could hope for."

From behind his back, the Grinch pulled out a single antler and presented it to Max with a flourish. "And that is why I'm promoting you! Max, you will guide my sleigh tonight!"

The Grinch balanced the antler on top of Max's head and tied it on with red string. "Can you feel the excitement?" he asked.

"ARF! ARF!" Max barked excitedly.

"Ha ha!" the Grinch laughed. "I knew you wouldn't let me down!"

The Grinch spent the rest of the day getting ready. He put together his Santa suit and tried it on, checking himself out in the mirror.

He liked what he saw!

And then, not a moment too soon for all the *Who* children (and their parents too, for that matter), it was Christmas Eve night.

Shopkeepers rushed to close their doors and hurry home. Everyone was eager to get inside their houses on the most magical night of the year.

And, for once, children were eager to go to bed.

In his room, Groopert looked out of the window, sitting next to his teddy bear, Mr Ruggles. "Now we have to stay awake," Groopert told his beloved bear. "Christmas history is about to be made." He crossed his fingers and hoped their plan worked – they'd given Cindy-Lou all the help they could.

Ozzy was in his own bedroom, running around in circles. Downstairs, his mother could hear his footsteps. *THUMP! THUMP! THUMP! THUMP!* "Ozzy, what are you DOING?" she yelled up to him.

"Trying to get myself tired!" he called down. "Phew!"

Izzy also wanted Christmas morning to come as soon as possible. She was already lying in bed, saying to herself, "All right. Eight hours until Christmas morning. That's 480 minutes, or 28,800 seconds. Okay. Aaaaaaand . . . sleep!"

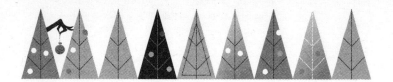

Axl knelt by his bed with his hands clasped together. "Please let me get what I want," he said quietly. "Please let me get what I want. Please let me get what I want."

One by one, the lights in *Who*-ville went off, until there was only one light left shining in the whole town.

19

The light was in Cindy-Lou *Who*'s bedroom. She sat up on her bed, staring out of the window at the starry sky. She was so excited. She could hardly wait for Santa to come flying over *Who*-ville in his magic sleigh. She'd be ready for him!

Her walkie-talkie buzzed, and Groopert's voice came through. "Waffle One, this is Waffle Two. Are you there? Over."

Cindy-Lou picked up her walkie-talkie and pressed the button. "I read you loud and clear, Waffle Two."

"This is Groopert, by the way."

"Yeah, I got that."

"Good luck tonight. I can't believe you're going to meet Santa Claus."

"Thanks!" Cindy-Lou said. "Talk tomorrow."

The door opened, and Donna came into Cindy-Lou's room. "So," she asked, smiling at her daughter staring out of the window, "have you got any last-minute wishes for Santa?"

"Yup," Cindy-Lou said, nodding her head. "I have one great big wish."

"Good," her mum said. "Because you deserve everything you want and more."

Cindy-Lou smiled back at her. "Thanks, Mum. I want the same thing for you."

Donna crossed the room and sat on the edge of Cindy-Lou's bed. "How did I end up with such a wonderful daughter?"

"I don't know," Cindy-Lou said, shrugging. "Sometimes you just get lucky."

"Well, then I really did."

"Me too."

They hugged. "I love you, Mum."

"I love you, sweetheart," Donna said. "Good night."

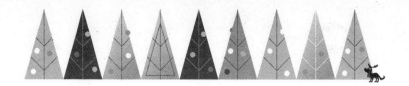

"Good night!" Cindy-Lou replied. Donna switched off the light and left.

After waiting a couple of moments, Cindy-Lou slipped out of bed and snuck out of her room. She had a trap to set.

Up on Mt. Crumpit, the Grinch climbed aboard his sleigh, full of purpose and confidence. He looked down at the quiet town of *Who*-ville, the target of his malicious plan. He took a deep breath, picked up the reins, and said, "Here we go, Max!"

He gave the reins a shake. Wearing his single antler, Max leaned into his harness, working his little legs back and forth with all his might. Instead of moving forward, he slowly disappeared down into the snow.

"Max!" cried the Grinch, looking at the spot where Max had just been standing. "Max, are you okay?"

After a moment, Max dug his way up out of the snow. He tried again, giving it everything he had. He pulled against the weight of the heavy sledge, slowly, slowly dragging it behind him down the mountain. As they inched forward, the Grinch laughed in triumph.

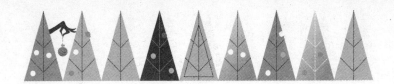

"Ha! Yes, Max! Attaboy! Go, boy, go!"

Picking up speed, the sleigh slid down the mountainside towards *Who*-ville and its twinkling Christmas lights. Soon, the Grinch and Max reached the town. They skimmed down a quiet street and came to a stop next to their first house. According to the route he'd marked on his model, the Grinch would begin stealing Christmas *right here*.

He hopped off the sleigh, and he and Max snuck closer to the house. "You take the outside," the Grinch whispered, "and I'll take the inside."

He pressed a button on Max's antler and – *CLICK* – a grappling hook popped out. Then he reached inside one of his bags and pressed another button. *SHUUUUUWOOP!* A ladder extended from the bag. The Grinch jumped on and rode the ladder up to the roof.

"Okay, house number one," he said as he crept across the snowy roof to the chimney. Using a set of helicopter-like rotary blades with a candy-cane handle, he floated down the chimney, through the fireplace, and out into the house. He barely even got any soot on his red Santa suit.

He landed in the middle of the living-room floor, turned off his candy cane and looked around. He took it all in – the tree, the presents, the decorations.

Satisfied, the Grinch smiled. "Okay. Now let's steal Christmas."

20

The Grinch started by sweeping the presents into bags with his big candy cane. Once he'd collected all the gifts, he took out a shrinking gadget he'd invented for just this purpose and aimed it at the bags – *ZZHWORK!* – instantly shrinking them down to a manageable size. Then he used his extending ladder to whisk the little bags up the chimney to the roof. One by one, they flew out of the chimney and landed in the snow. *PLOP! PLOP! PLOP!*

Meanwhile, outside the house, Max was using the grappling hook attached to his head to strip all the Christmas lights from

the roof and windows. Within seconds he'd removed every single bulb and cord. The house was now dark.

Back inside, the Grinch tossed martial arts throwing stars – *ZWICK! ZWICK! ZWICK!* – at the Christmas tree, tying it into a bundle before sending it up the chimney and on to the roof.

The Grinch looked around the room. He'd successfully picked the whole house clean in a matter of seconds. There wasn't a single sign of Christmas cheer to be seen anywhere! He grinned an evil grin and rode his ladder up the chimney to the roof, pulling it up behind him. *ZWIP!*

This was the moment when the extendo-shoes he'd invented came in handy. By extending them, he could simply walk from one roof to the next! In no time at all, he was down the next house's chimney and into the living room.

For a moment, he stood with two candy canes crossed in front of his chest. Then, with a move he'd practised back in his cave, he used the candy canes to throw nets round all the presents piled under the tree. He reeled them in like a big school of fish.

For extra speed, the Grinch rode a tricycle before he bagged it up, zipping past a delicious-looking cookie set out on a table for

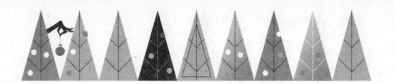

Santa. But he stuck to his training – he would not be distracted!

Soon he'd cleaned out the second house. He and Max moved on to the next, and the next, and the next . . .

Using his clever inventions, the Grinch, together with Max, moved faster and faster, zooming from house to house, leaving each one picked clean behind them.

Each time they finished a house, a counter on the sleigh ticked down by one. 154, 153, 152, 151 . . . Until finally, after several hours of night-time thievery, the counter on the sleigh clicked down to 001. In all of *Who*-ville, there was only one house left with Christmas presents, stockings and decorations.

Cindy-Lou *Who*'s house.

The Grinch and Max pulled up to the house in the sleigh. It was easy to spot, because it was the last house in *Who*-ville that still bore any sign of Christmas, including a glimpse through the window of a beautiful tree covered in lights and decorations.

"This is it!" the Grinch said, grinning. "The last house."

Savouring the moment, he climbed out of the sleigh, absentmindedly giving Max a pat. Then he reached down and pressed a button on his extendo-shoes. *CLICK-CLICK-*

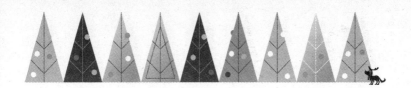

CLICKETY-CLICK-CLACK! The built-in ladders extended, shooting him up to the roof. He relished the winter wind blowing in his face as he rose to the top of the house.

He crossed the roof, leaving a trail of extendo-shoe prints in the snow. Pulling out his candy-cane propeller, he climbed up on to the chimney and floated down it into the house.

The Grinch popped out of the fireplace and looked around. He started with the tree, wrapping it up with wires and preparing to send the bundle up the chimney. Then, across the room, he noticed something . . . an extremely delicious-looking, beautifully decorated Christmas biscuit sitting on a plate. It had obviously been left out for Santa.

"Ah, what a gorgeous biscuit," he said to himself. Then he remembered his lecture to Max and Fred. Even in the face of great temptation, one must remain disciplined! One must resist!

But that had just been to make sure they hit all the houses in one night. And they'd done it! Surely, having done such an incredible job of thievery, he deserved just one little biscuit!

"Oh, what the heck," the Grinch said as he crossed the room to the plate.

He snatched the beautiful biscuit and – *Wha!* – Cindy-Lou's trap was sprung! A WELCOME, SANTA! sign swung into place, dangling on strings.

Up in Cindy-Lou's bedroom, a bell over her bed rang. *DING-A-LING-A-LING!* She instantly woke up (just as Groopert had suspected, she hadn't been able to stay awake either).

"It worked!" she said in an excited whisper. "My trap worked!"

21

Bright lights blazed on all round the WELCOME, SANTA! sign. *FWOOOM!* Blinded by them, the Grinch stumbled back. But as he did so, a rope wrapped round his furry green ankle and yanked the Grinch up towards the ceiling! "AAAAAHHH!" he yelled.

Upstairs, a light snapped on. Dangling in the air, the Grinch looked up at it, panicking. He mustn't be caught stealing Christmas!

Cindy-Lou peeked down over the bannister. "Santa Claus," she said quietly, amazed that her plan had actually worked.

The Grinch kept shifting and wiggling, hoping to break free. Maybe he could still run away without having to talk to anyone! But then he spotted Cindy-Lou tiptoeing cautiously down the stairs.

"Oh, hello," the Grinch said, trying to sound casual and calm, the way he imagined a little girl might think Santa would sound. "Could you give me a little help, please?"

"I'll let you down," Cindy-Lou assured him. "Just give me a minute!"

"Ah, that would be great," the Grinch said.

Cindy-Lou hurried the rest of the way down the staircase, saying, "I'm coming! Just trying to remember which is the release cord!" When she reached the bottom of the stairs, she undid her trap. *THUMP!* The Grinch fell from the ceiling and hit the floor.

"There we go!" Cindy-Lou said, running to help untangle him from the rope. She handed him the glass of milk by the biscuit plate. "Drink this. It'll make you feel better."

The Grinch waved off the milk. He just wanted to get out of there!

"Santa, I know you're busy," she said, repeating the words

she'd rehearsed dozens of times, preparing for just this moment. "But there's something really important that I need . . ."

Suddenly Cindy-Lou stopped her speech. She'd noticed something: their beautiful Christmas tree, bound by netting and stuffed partway up the chimney! "Wait," she said, confused. "Why are you taking our Christmas tree?"

The Grinch stood up, busted. Could he just run away? No, that wouldn't do. He had to think, and he had to think quickly. Why would Santa stuff a perfectly good Christmas tree up a chimney? "Well," he improvised, "one of the lights on your tree wasn't working, so I thought I'd take it back to my workshop and see if I could fix it."

"I didn't know you did that," Cindy-Lou said. She'd heard a lot of stories about Santa Claus, but none of them had included light-bulb repair.

"All the time. Just a little service I like to provide. Call me a perfectionist. Now why don't you go back upstairs to bed, and then when you wake up, the tree will be fixed and your presents will be waiting under it."

He tried to turn Cindy-Lou around and scoot her back towards the stairway.

"Wait, you don't understand," she said, resisting. "I don't want presents."

"Of course you do," the Grinch insisted, gently pushing her along. "Everyone wants presents."

"No, no, really I don't," Cindy-Lou said, slipping away and turning back to face him. "I want you to help my mum!"

The Grinch looked surprised. "Your mum?"

"Yeah," Cindy-Lou said, getting back to her original script. "She works so hard and is always doing stuff for other people . . . and my brothers . . . and me. And I just want her to be happy."

Stunned, the Grinch stared at the little *Who*. He'd always thought *Whos* only cared about the presents they got each Christmas. The thoughtfulness of Cindy-Lou's request touched him, but he was so unfamiliar with the feeling that he didn't even realise that's what was happening. "You want me to help your mum?" he repeated.

Cindy-Lou nodded, smiling up at him. "You're Santa. You make people happy. And everyone should be happy, right?"

The Grinch was so surprised by this whole conversation that he really had no idea what to say. He just stood there, looking into

Cindy-Lou's big eyes. "Yeah," he finally muttered. "I guess they should."

To Cindy-Lou, Santa sounded sad. "Santa, are you okay?" she asked.

The Grinch had been thinking about how he had never really been happy, not even when he was a little Grinch. "What? Me?" he said, clearing his throat and trying to sound cheerful. "I'm fine! Now why don't you go back to bed, okay?"

"Okay," Cindy-Lou agreed. She'd said what she'd planned to say; she couldn't do anything more. Now it was up to Santa to see what he could do to help her mum.

The Grinch ushered her towards the steps. She hurried up a few and then turned round, worried about how sad Santa had seemed. "I wish you could celebrate with us tomorrow," she said. "We all get together and sing. And it's so beautiful that if you close your eyes and listen, all your sadness just goes away." She closed her eyes, remembering other Christmases.

The Grinch looked at the little *Who* standing on the stairway with her eyes closed. "That sounds nice," he said. And he meant it. It did sound nice.

"Good night," Cindy-Lou said. She leaned forward and hugged the Grinch. "Thank you, Santa. For everything."

The Grinch just stood there. When was the last time anyone had hugged him? Had anyone ever hugged him?

"Good night," he said quietly.

22

When Cindy-Lou was back upstairs in her bed, the Grinch, lost in thought, mechanically turned back to the tree and stuffed it the rest of the way up the chimney. Then he used his candy cane to rise up the chimney himself.

Up on the roof, he slid the last sack and the tree down to Max, who was waiting in the garden below. The Grinch used his extendo-shoes to step off the roof and lower himself to the ground. He climbed into the sleigh and looked around at the darkened houses of *Who*-ville.

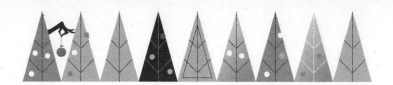

He'd done it. He'd stolen Christmas. So why didn't he feel triumphant? Gleeful? Deliciously mean?

"I just met the strangest little *Who* girl," the Grinch told Max.

His loyal dog looked back at him, concerned. What was the matter with his master?

The Grinch shook himself and clicked the counter down to zero. "All right, Max," he said, picking up the reins. "Let's go."

Straining, Max leaned into his harness, taking one step at a time and slowly inching forward. It helped that the streets of *Who*-ville were slippery with ice and snow. Soon the loaded sleigh was making its way through the dark and cheerless town.

As he rode towards the base of Mt. Crumpit, the Grinch couldn't stop thinking about what the little *Who* girl had said. Could it really be that simple? Could closing your eyes and listening to a song really make all your sadness go away?

Early the next morning, as the sun rose over the snowy town of *Who*-ville, Cindy-Lou sat up in bed and rubbed the sleep from

her eyes. Suddenly, her brain kicked in and she remembered: it was Christmas morning! *CHRISTMAS!*

She jumped out of bed and ran downstairs to the living room.

Empty! No presents, no decorations, no tree.

"What?" she asked, stunned. She stood there, staring, unable to believe what she was seeing. Was this some kind of cruel joke?

Smiling, Donna walked into the living room. But when she saw everything gone, her smile disappeared. "Oh no!" she said. "What happened?"

That was exactly what every *Who* in town wanted to know. They wandered out of their houses in shock. As they looked around, they saw that the Christmas decorations and lights had disappeared from the outsides of their houses, too. All of it – gone!

Instinctively, everyone headed towards the town square. Passing all the undecorated houses and shops, everyone was asking themselves the same question: who could have done such an awful, nasty thing?

As she stood in the centre of the square with the other sad and bewildered *Whos*, Cindy-Lou realised she just might know the answer to that question.

Up on Mt. Crumpit, the Grinch and Max were dragging the overloaded sleigh to the very top of the very highest, tip-top peak. When they got there, they were going to shove the sleigh over the edge. It would plummet through the crisp morning air and land on the jagged rocks far below, where no one could possibly retrieve it. Every present, every tree and every decoration would be smashed and broken. Christmas, at least for one year, would disappear in a single big crash.

"Keep going, Max," the Grinch said, full of grim determination. "We're almost there – we're going to make it."

The *Whos* kept pouring into the town square. Cindy-Lou spotted her friends looking dumbfounded.

"Oh dear," Ozzy said when he saw that the decorations were even gone from the square.

"What happened?" Izzy asked.

"Where are the decorations?" Ozzy asked.

"All the presents?" Groopert muttered.

"Aw, man," Axl said sadly.

Cindy-Lou just bowed her head, not knowing what to say. She turned to Donna. "Mum," she said, "it's my fault."

Donna looked puzzled. "What is?"

"All of this," Cindy-Lou said, gesturing towards the undecorated square and all the shocked citizens. "I trapped Santa last night so I could talk to him, and it must have made him so mad he stole everyone's Christmas."

Donna put her hands on her daughter's shoulders and knelt down, moving her face close to Cindy-Lou's. "No, honey," she said, shaking her head. "This isn't your fault. Whoever did this didn't steal Christmas, he just stole stuff. Christmas is here." She pointed to her daughter's heart. "And no one can steal that."

Standing up, Donna held her hand out to her daughter. After a moment, Cindy-Lou took it. Then she offered her other hand to Groopert. He took her hand, and extended his other hand to Izzy. All the *Whos* in *Who*-ville began to join hands one by one.

23

Up on Mt. Crumpit, the sleigh containing the presents and decorations was teetering on the edge of the mountain, ready to fall. The Grinch put his shoulder against it. "Just one more shove," he said.

But at that moment, a faint sound drifted up the mountain from *Who*-ville far below. As it grew louder, the Grinch strained to make sense of the noise.

"What's that?" he asked Max, cupping a hand to his ear. "Do you hear it?"

When he realised exactly what he was hearing, the Grinch was flabbergasted. "They're . . . singing!" he said.

He was right. The sound of hundreds of happy *Whos* raising their voices to sing a Christmas carol together floated right up the mountain to the Grinch's furry green ears.

The Grinch couldn't believe it. How could they be singing a joyous song together? He'd stolen their Christmas! This was not what he'd expected! Crying and wailing? Yes! Singing? No!

"I don't understand, Max," he said.

The Grinch climbed carefully on to the sleigh that was stacked with sacks of presents. Searching through the bags, he found a small telescope tied with a bow. He hurried over to the edge of a rocky outcropping and put the telescope to his eye, pointing the other end at *Who*-ville.

The Grinch saw all the *Whos* standing in a big circle, holding hands. Their mouths moved in perfect unison as they sang together. And they looked so . . . happy!

"Don't they know what I've done?" the Grinch asked, lowering the telescope. Max shrugged.

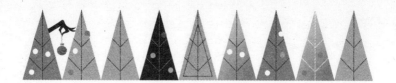

The Grinch took another look, scanning the crowd until he found Cindy-Lou *Who*. Her eyes were closed, and she smiled as she sang, lifting her face towards the sky. He heard her little voice in his head, saying, "It's so beautiful that if you close your eyes and listen, all your sadness just goes away."

Could it be true?

The Grinch lowered the telescope again. He listened carefully to the sound of the *Whos* singing together. And he felt something – something strong, deep and profound.

Max looked up at his master. What was he doing?

Closing his eyes, the Grinch tilted his head back, letting the music flow into him. He smiled. When he listened to the music with his heart, he felt it surge . . . and swell . . . until it grew three sizes! His sadness went away! He felt a joy he'd never experienced in his whole life. Bliss! And then he realised something else . . .

THE SLEIGH WAS ABOUT TO FALL OVER THE CLIFF!

"Wha—?" he cried. "OH NO!"

As the sleigh wobbled on the edge, the Grinch jumped up and grabbed the back end. He tried to stop the sleigh from falling,

but it was too heavy for him. It toppled over the edge, taking the Grinch with it! "YAAAAH!" the Grinch screamed.

Thinking quickly, the Grinch whipped out his candy cane, aimed it back up the mountain and pressed a button. *SHWOOMP!* A grappling hook shot out of the end of the candy cane and snagged the edge of the cliff. Max peered down, looking worried.

"It's okay, Max," the Grinch said. "I'm going to—"

The rocky cliff started to crumble under the grappling hook.

"AHHH!" the Grinch shouted. "Oh, no, no, no!"

CRRRACK! The edge of the cliff broke off. The Grinch began to fall . . .

"MAAAAAX!" he screamed.

But then there was a tug on the grappling hook's rope! The Grinch looked up . . . and saw Fred and his family pulling on it! Max was helping too. Working together, they pulled the Grinch and the sleigh back up to safety.

"Fred?" the Grinch said, walking towards the reindeer, amazed. "You came back!"

Then the Grinch looked towards *Who*-ville, full of resolve. "Come on, Max, my boy!"

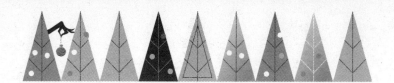

He jumped up into the driver's seat. As the sleigh began to slide down the side of the mountain in the direction of Who-ville, the Grinch scooped up Max and set him on the seat next to him.

"ARF! ARF!" the little dog barked, wagging his tail. He was very happy to be riding instead of pulling. And the Grinch was happy to have Max with him.

As the sleigh picked up speed, the Grinch grabbed a horn, climbed on to the stack of presents, and blew it as loudly as he could to let the Whos know he was coming. *FA-WAAAH! FA-WOOO! FA-FA-FA-WAAAAAAH!*

The Grinch was determined to make things right. "I hope we haven't lost anyone's presents, Max," he said. The smile on Max's face said that everything would be all right.

Down in the town square, one of the Whos opened their eyes and shouted – he'd spotted the tall stack of Christmas gifts and decorations heading through town, coming right towards them! The other Whos turned to see the approaching tower of presents, and one by one, the Whos stopped singing. They opened up their circle so the Grinch could slide right into the middle.

"Uh, hello, everybody," he said awkwardly after the sleigh

had come to a stop. "I've come to return your gifts. I stole your Christmas. Because . . ." He paused. Why *had* he stolen their Christmas, exactly? "Because I thought it would fix something that happened a long time ago."

The *Whos* looked surprised. That's not what they'd expected the mean old Grinch to say.

"But it didn't," he admitted. "And I'm sorry."

The Grinch spotted Cindy-Lou in the crowd. He walked over to her. "I'm so very sorry. For everything."

Slumping his shoulders, the Grinch turned and began to walk away, heading back towards his lonely cave, his loyal friend Max following after him.

24

ack up on Mt. Crumpit, the Grinch entered his cave and headed down a hallway. Max tried to follow, but the Grinch stopped him. "Not now, Max," he said. "I need to be alone."

Max trotted off down another corridor to his bed. As he lay on the little mattress, he stared at the framed picture of the Grinch and him and sighed.

DING-A-LING! The bell rang, summoning Max. He sprang up, climbed the steps, and jumped on to the platform that pushed down into the vat of coffee, pouring out a cup. He perched the tray on his head, and balanced the cup of hot coffee on the tray.

But as he started to back into the little lift that would carry him up to the Grinch's bedroom, he saw something.

Inside the lift was a new ball with a shiny Christmas bow on it!

"I thought you might like it," came the Grinch's voice from behind him "If you don't, I can take it back. It's not a big deal. I just thought maybe you'd—"

"ARF! ARF!" Max barked happily. He began playing with the ball, batting it with his paws and then jumping on it, biting it.

"Oh! Heh," the Grinch said, smiling. "Merry Christmas to you, too, Max."

SQUEAK! SQUEAK! Every time Max bit the ball, it squeaked. *SQUEAK!*

"That's going to get old," the Grinch said, rolling his eyes.

KNOCK! KNOCK!

"What was that?" the Grinch said, turning towards the sound. It had been so long since anyone had knocked on the cave's front door that the Grinch had forgotten what it sounded like.

KNOCK! KNOCK!

It was definitely a knock at the front door. But who could be knocking?

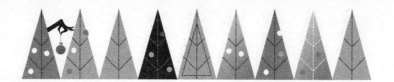

He made his way to the front door, opened it and looked outside, expecting to see a furious crowd. But all he saw was Cindy-Lou *Who* standing in the snow, staring up at him with her big, round eyes.

"Uh . . . hello," the Grinch said, surprised.

"Hi!" Cindy-Lou said brightly. "Remember me?"

"Yes," the Grinch replied. "Yes, I do. I remember you."

She stuck out her small hand. "My name is Cindy-Lou. Cindy-Lou *Who.*"

"It's nice to meet you, Cindy-Lou," the Grinch said, shaking her hand. "My name is Grinch."

Down by the Grinch's feet, Max squeezed his new ball. *SQUEAK!* "And, uh, this is Max," the Grinch added.

"Whoa! Nice to meet you, Max!" Cindy-Lou said, laughing as he licked her face. She looked back up at the Grinch. "I just came to invite you to our house for Christmas dinner."

"What?" the Grinch said. "Me? But I took your gifts!"

"Yeah," Cindy-Lou said, nodding. "I know."

"And your trees," the Grinch said.

"Yup," Cindy-Lou agreed.

"I stole your whole Christmas," the Grinch reminded her.

"I know you did," she said. "But we're inviting you anyway."

The Grinch didn't understand. "But why?" he asked, utterly bewildered.

"Because," Cindy-Lou explained, "you've been alone long enough."

She turned, walked to her sledge, and started back down the mountain, calling, "Dinner's at six! Don't be late! And make sure you bring Max, too!"

The Grinch watched her go. An invitation to Christmas dinner? He'd never been invited to a Christmas dinner in his life!

At six o'clock that evening, the Grinch stood outside the front door of the house where Cindy-Lou lived with her mother and twin brothers. He wore a black tie over his green suit. His hair was neatly combed. Max was with him.

He was terrified.

He slowly moved his shaking finger towards the doorbell, then yanked it back. He tried again, but failed. "Bad idea," he muttered to himself. "I can't do this. I can't do this!"

25

But he did. He took a deep breath and rang the bell. *DING-DONG!*

"Here we go," he said to Max.

The door swung open. Donna stood in the doorway holding a big bowl with a whisk in it. "Oh, Mr Grinch!" she said. "I'm so glad you could make it!"

"Uh, h-hi," the Grinch stammered nervously. "I wore a tie."

Donna smiled. "It's a very nice tie." She turned and called back into the house, "Cindy-Lou, look who's here!"

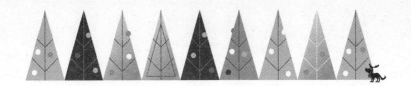

Cindy-Lou ran to the front door, squeezing in beside her mum to greet the Grinch. "Mr Grinch! You came!" she said. "Come on," she went on, taking him by the hand. "I'll introduce you to everyone!"

Cindy-Lou led the Grinch through the party. Lots of *Whos* had come for dinner. One of them put her hand on the Grinch's shoulder. He whipped round, startled.

"Hello, Mr Grinch," she said warmly. "Merry Christmas!"

"Merry Christmas to you too," the Grinch said, surprised.

"Aunt Ida," Cindy-Lou said, "I'd like you to meet my friend the Grinch."

"It's nice to meet you, Mr Grinch," Aunt Ida said.

"Thank you," the Grinch answered. "It's nice to be here." He smiled nervously.

Donna entered with a big tray of appetisers. "Cindy-Lou? Could you make a little room for this tray?"

"I'll do that," the Grinch offered. "Let me help you." He took the tray and found a spot for it.

"Oh!" Donna said. "Thank you!"

The Grinch saw several kids playing with Max, and smiled

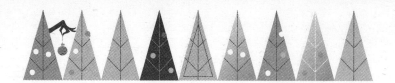

again. Then he heard a familiar voice. "Is that grouchy, grumpy Grinchy I see standing over there?"

"Bricklebaum!" the Grinch exclaimed. "Good to see you!" To his surprise he found it *was* good to see a familiar friendly face.

Bricklebaum hurried over. "Come on, Grinchy! Give me a hug!" He grabbed the Grinch in a hearty bear hug that lifted him off the ground. "It doesn't count if you don't hug back, buddy!"

"Come and take your seats everyone!" Donna called from the dining room. "Dinner's ready!"

Laughing and chatting, the crowd of guests hurried into the dining room, chose seats and sat down. Delicious smells came from the dishes on the big round table.

"Come on," Cindy-Lou said, taking the Grinch's hand again. "You're sitting next to me." She guided him to an empty chair and sat down next to him. All round the table, *Whos* were smiling and talking, ready to eat.

Under the table, Max was having a great time playing with Mabel, who went everywhere with Bricklebaum. Later, he'd be sneaking little bits of food to her – and to Max, too.

Everyone seemed completely relaxed. Everyone, that is,

except the Grinch, who still felt uncomfortable in these unfamiliar surroundings. "This is my first Christmas dinner," the Grinch confided nervously to Cindy-Lou. "What happens?"

"You'll see," Cindy-Lou assured him.

Through the door from the kitchen came Donna, carrying a big platter with a beautiful Roast Beast on it. The Grinch remembered gazing from the outside as *Who* families sat down to their Christmas dinners. Now he was on the inside. He watched as she stopped and set the platter down right in front of him.

"Would you do the honours, please, Mr Grinch?"

"Me?" he asked, amazed.

Donna nodded, smiling.

"Okay," he agreed. He reached for the big carving knife and fork. But, before he started, he pushed back his chair and stood up. "Do you mind if I say something first?"

"Not at all," Donna said.

"Well," the Grinch began, "um, well, everybody. I just want to say that I've spent my entire life hating Christmas and everything about it."

The *Whos* stared at him.

"But now," he continued, "I see it wasn't Christmas that I hated." He swallowed. "It was being alone." He took a breath and stood up a little straighter. "But I'm not alone any more." He looked out at everyone seated round the big table and smiled. "And I have all of you to thank for it." Then he turned to Cindy-Lou, sitting in the chair next to his, looking up at him. "And especially this little girl right here." He turned to Donna. "Ms *Who*, your daughter's kindness changed my life."

Donna hugged Cindy-Lou. "That's my girl," she said.

"Oh, that was beautiful," Bricklebaum said, brushing away a tear. He turned to the *Who* seated next to him and whispered, "That's my best friend."

"Merry Christmas, Mr Grinch," Cindy-Lou said, smiling.

"Merry Christmas, Cindy-Lou," the Grinch said.

The Grinch raised his glass. Everyone round the table raised theirs, too, joining him in a Christmas toast.

"To kindness and love," he said, "the things we need most."

And with that, the Grinch began to serve the slices of Roast Beast to his new friends.

Celebrate with these other festive feasts . . .

ILLUMINATION PRESENTS
Dr. Seuss'
The
GRINCH

MOVIE
STICKER
BOOK

PACKED WITH
250 STICKERS AND
FESTIVE THINGS TO
MAKE—AND—DO!

ILLUMINATION PRESENTS

Dr. Seuss'

The GRINCH

MOVIE
COLOURING
BOOK

BASED ON THE FUNNY,
HEARTWARMING
NEW MOVIE